A Rosslyn Treasury

Stories and Legends from Rosslyn Chapel

A Rosslyn Treasury

Stories and Legends from Rosslyn Chapel

P. L. Snow

Floris Books

First published in English by Floris Books in 2009

British CIP Data available

ISBN 978-086315-710-3

Printed in Great Britain
by Bell & Bain, Glasgow.

To Mary with love and thanks.

My heartfelt thanks are due to Christian Maclean of Floris Books, for first suggesting the idea of a book about Rosslyn; to Christopher Moore, my editor, whose advice and guidance were wise, kind and invaluable; to the staff of Rosslyn Chapel, for their cheery helpfulness; and my family, who supported and encouraged me throughout.

Contents

Rosslyn and its Stories and Legends

This is a collection of stories, all of which are inspired by Rosslyn Chapel. The many carvings in the chapel represent stories, and here, many of those tales are retold. They come from ancient myth and legend, from Biblical sources, and from traditions close to the Bible, such as the tales of Jewish folklore, collected by Micha Joseph bin Gorion. Some of them come from Scottish and European history and others from more modern sources. As diverse as they are, they are a testament to the richness of the culture that Rosslyn represents.

Rosslyn Chapel stands some eight miles south of Edinburgh. At first sight, it is a fairly small, gothic construction, rather dark and perhaps even forbidding-looking. On entering, though, the first impression is of a building larger on the inside than the outside. The ceiling seems higher than the outside suggests, and the stained-glass windows brighter and more colourful. Looking eastwards, the arches of the Lady Chapel, with their strange rhomboidal protuberances, seem unwelcoming, as though guarding a secret, like a sort of barbed-wire fence for the imagination, keeping it at bay. Rosslyn is famous for keeping its secrets!

For many, even today, when the idea of a pilgrimage could be thought to belong to an earlier time, Rosslyn is a stage on the pilgrimage to Santiago de Compostela, in the north-west of Spain. This journey goes by way of Chartres Cathedral, near Paris, and many of Rosslyn's carvings have their counterpart in Chartres. In the past, on their return, the pilgrims would place the token of their journey, a cockle shell, on a pile with others. The shells would then be ground up into the mortar that holds the chapel together.

The awakened face and the Recording Angel: the beginning of pilgrimage.

The postulant led to the place of initiation. The carving is much weathered and worn, but the blindfold and cord round his neck are still visible.

But what, after all, is a pilgrimage? Perhaps we can think of it as a journey, usually to a place with particular spiritual resonance. To undertake this journey means that the traveller wishes to *change* something within him or herself; both to deepen his or her own spiritual awareness, and to be able to penetrate more fully the significance of the place of pilgrimage on arrival. The journey is as important as its end, as it is the conscious preparation for the arrival. Many of the stories here involve such journeys.

A long tradition links Rosslyn Chapel with the Templar Knights. Indeed, there are signs in the chapel that indicate a connection, even though the chapel was not begun until over a century after the Templars had been harried out of existence through the machinations of a vengeful and avaricious king. The links and traditions that bind Rosslyn to the Templars mean that their story must be told here.

Rosslyn is also connected in many people's minds with the Holy Grail, especially after the publication of Dan Brown's book, *The Da Vinci Code* — not to mention the film based on the book, shot partly on location at Rosslyn. The Grail has engaged the imaginations of people for over a thousand years. Naturally, there is a chapter here that considers that mysterious subject.

Some themes seem to recur throughout the stories: initiation practices; the Sons of the Widow; the Templar Knights themselves. Historical personages appear, sometimes as pilgrims following their journey through life, sometimes as less admirable individuals.

In recent years, Rosslyn has appeared as the background to newer stories. I have followed this trend in two stories, one of which, *A Fantasy of Rosslyn*, includes an account of a Rose-Cross initiation, such as is hinted at in a particular carving in the chapel. It should, however, be made clear that this description comes from a time shortly before the Rosicrucians — the followers of that extraordinary individual Christian Rosenkreutz — began their work in the world. It seems to me unlikely, though, that there should be no connection at all between the Rose-Cross depicted in the chapel and the symbol of Christian Rosenkreutz. The final tale, *The Last of the Templars*, is based on a true story that I discovered during my research for this book.

Here, then, are myths, legends and other tales inspired directly by that remarkable building, Rosslyn Chapel. I hope you enjoy them, and even that, if you have not already done so, you might visit the chapel, perhaps even to find new stories of your own.

A Brief History of Rosslyn

The Sinclairs of Rosslyn

The Sinclairs, who built Rosslyn Chapel, came originally from Norway, tracing their descent from Rognvald of Moere. A branch of the family settled in Normandy, at Saint Clair-sur-Epte, whence they took their Norman-French name, Saint Clair. They arrived in Britain with William the Conqueror in 1066, but some members of the family travelled north, and found fame and honour in Scotland.

The Barony of Roslin, or at least, a goodly portion of it, was given to one William 'the Seemly', a member of the Sinclair family, by King Malcolm Canmore in life rental, at first, at the end of the eleventh century.*

This William Sinclair, along with the Hungarian knight Ladislaus Lecelin, had been part of the escort for Margaret, the Saxon princess and descendant of King Alfred the Great. She later married Malcolm Canmore, and a chapter in the book tells her story. Ladislaus Lecelin remained in Scotland to become the progenitor of the clan Leslie. The whole barony was given to the Sinclair family as free heritage by Malcolm and Margaret's youngest son, King David I, as a reward for helping to protect the border against English invasion.

---

* The spelling 'Roslin' refers to the town, and sometimes the castle; 'Rosslyn' to the chapel. There are other variants, for instance, Rosling, Roscelyn; but we adhere to the most common versions.

Some two hundred years later, another William Sinclair, the third Earl of Orkney, succeeded his father in 1417. He was very young at the time; no more than six or seven. Father Richard Hay, whose mother, after becoming widowed, married Sir James Sinclair of Rosslyn, devoted a great deal of his time to studying various documents in possession of the Sinclair family, and gave us probably the best early history of the family and the chapel extant. Writing in the seventeenth century, he tells us that the third Earl:

> ... his age creeping on him ... made him consider how
> he had spent his time past, and how to spend that
> which was to come ... (It) came into his minde to build
> a house for God's service, of most curious worke ...

This 'house for God's work' was of course Rosslyn Chapel. The date that Father Hay gives for the commencement of the work is 1446. That was the year in which permission was given for the building to commence on a site near Roslin Castle, of what had been an ancient centre of Mithras worship during Roman times.

The building of the chapel

It seems that it was originally intended that the final building should be a much larger construction. However, Earl William died in 1484, and his son Oliver did not carry out the design for the larger building, but made sure, simply, that the structure be finished off in the state in which William left it at his death. Oliver's son made sure that lands were available for houses and gardens for the provost and prebendaries. That, at any rate, is one version of the story. Others hold that Rosslyn was never intended to become the great cathedral building that was projected, but was built with a different purpose.

The work ended in 1487. Thus the chapel was forty years in construction, like the Temple of Solomon, as we know from the Gospel of John. Perhaps this alone was a hint to Oliver Sinclair that no more work needed to be done: a temple of a sort was accomplished.

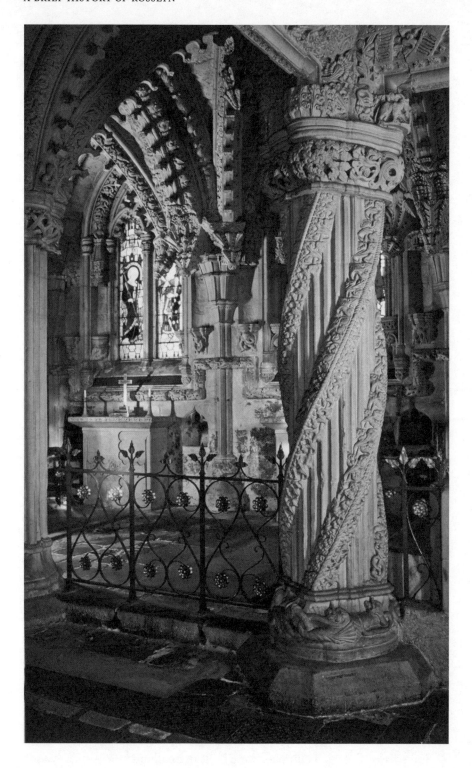

The Apprentice pillar.

Earl William employed a number of masons, smiths, carpenters and others. The carvings were first made in wood; approval for the designs was sought from Sinclair, or his colleague in the guidance of the building, Sir Gilbert de la Haye; then, if approval was given, the masons copied the designs in stone and fixed them into the fabric of the building. In the words of Father Hay:

> He rewarded the massones according to their degree, as
> to the master massone he gave forty pounds yearly, and
> to everyone of the rest ten pounds, and accordingly did
> he reward the others, as the smiths and the carpenters
> with others.

Mark Oxbrow and Ian Robertson in *Rosslyn and the Grail* and Alan Butler and John Ritchie in *Rosslyn Revealed* point to the importance of Sir Gilbert de la Haye in the construction and indeed the conception of the chapel. Sir Gilbert was a scholar, educated at Saint Andrews University, and had served in France in the Garde Écossaise, in support of Joan of Arc. He was a gifted linguist, and commissioned by Earl William to translate various works of chivalry. Oxbrow and Robertson go so far as to suggest that the idea of building the chapel came originally from Sir Gilbert and the Earl's wife, Elizabeth Douglas. Many scholars are agreed that the influence of Lady Elizabeth on the early construction of the chapel was very strong. However, she died in 1451, shortly after work on the chapel began. Her coat of arms is to be seen in the Lower Chapel, or crypt, together with her husband's. In another place in the crypt, Earl William's coat of arms stands alone, and in yet a third place, we see his arms together with that of his second wife, Marjorie Sutherland.

Sir Gilbert and Earl William, between them, possessed a formidable amount of esoteric knowledge. Dr Tim Wallace-Murphy, in his book *Rosslyn — Guardian of the Secrets of the Holy Grail* describes Earl William as 'one of the Illuminati ... an adept of highest degree', while the books written and translated by Sir Gilbert show that he, too, was something of an initiate.

Already by 1456, the structure at Rosslyn was known as a 'College Kirk', or Collegiate Church. The word 'collegiate', however, does not necessarily imply the existence of some sort of group of people banded together in some worthy enterprise.

Some forty-five such churches were built in Scotland 'to ensure salvation for the founder and his family by providing for prayers to be offered in perpetuity by a succession of Priests.' (Richard Fawcett, *Scottish Architecture 1371–1560.*) All that was finished of Rosslyn, though, was the quire, the 'head' as it were, of a cruciform building; the easternmost part of the structure. Christopher Knight and Robert Lomas argue in some of their books that this was quite intentional, and that the resulting structure was an imaginative reworking of the Temple of Solomon, with all that that suggests for the Craft of Freemasonry. Others remain extremely sceptical about this. Whether Rosslyn Chapel is a highly imaginative reworking of Solomon's Temple or not, it is *very* similar to the quire of Saint Mungo's Cathedral in Glasgow, though Saint Mungo's is much bigger, and has nothing of the carving that makes Rosslyn so interesting.

Earl William's difficulties were increased in the 1450s and 1460s, and it appears that there were fewer funds available to him. Between 1468 and 1470 he lost the majority of his Orkney earldom. Thus it seems likely that he was, in fact, struggling financially at this period. Indeed, if Rosslyn is an unfinished Collegiate Church, it is not alone. There are others that never reached completion, for various reasons. But even in its unfinished state, a provost and prebendaries — that is, priests attached to the chapel — were put in place to make sure that the Holy Offices were observed regularly, in common with other Collegiate churches in Scotland.

The Reformation

The chapel became a Roman Catholic church during the early part of the sixteenth century, but with the Protestant Reformation, it suffered a great deal of damage. John Knox, the reforming prelate, mentioned with some bitterness during the 1560s to his congregation on one occasion that Mary Queen of Scots was in the habit of hearing mass either at Rosslyn or at Woodhouselee, while she was resident at Craigmillar Castle. It was not long before Knox's hearers marched on Rosslyn Chapel intent on destruction, calling the place 'a house and monument of idolatrie'. It is said that they hauled down statues of the Apostles from the niches above the nave, and smashed them up. Luckily, a local farmer by the name of Thomas Cochrane told the mob that the nearby castle cellars were full of good wine. The image-smashers gladly abandoned their work and made for the castle. The loss of the statuary is grave, but thanks to Tam Cochrane, the damage was not worse.

In spite of the reforming zeal of the times, the Sinclair family of Roslin had remained Catholic for some fifty years after the Reformation. The Provost and the prebendaries of the chapel had resigned in 1571; this is not surprising when one learns that their endowments, which had been withheld on a regular basis, were now taken from them 'by force and violence', and their homes vandalized by the mob. In August 1592, the stone altars in the chapel were dragged out and destroyed. The destruction of the altars 'till one stane or tua hight' (to the height of one or two stones) clearly did nothing to reconcile Sir William Sinclair — yet another of that name — to the new Protestant Church of Scotland. He was accused of not attending his parish church in Lasswade, as the law demanded; but he argued that he was resident in another parish that had no minister. On being asked about the baptism of one of his children, he replied that he did not know whether the child was baptized or not. This child was probably illegitimate, and Sir William was given the reputation of being a lewd man, who kept a miller's daughter as a mistress. When summoned to do penance for fornication, he refused to sit on the 'creepy stool' for every such offence, but indicated that he would consider sitting if he was given a quart of wine to pass the time. Finally, Sir William and his girlfriend left Scotland for Ireland, hoping to find life more amenable to Catholics there.

By the seventeenth century, Rosslyn was now no longer considered a place fit for Christian worship. When General Monk came north to fire on Roslin Castle in 1650, on behalf of the forces sympathetic to Oliver Cromwell, the chapel was used as a stable for the General's horses. This was the same year in which another Sir William Sinclair fell at the Battle of Dunbar, and was the last of his family to be laid to rest in his armour beneath the floor of the chapel. This at least indicates that the chapel was still of considerable importance to the family as a mausoleum, if not a place of worship.

Again, in 1688, a Protestant mob attacked the chapel, defacing the carvings. Even though it was no longer recognized as a House of God, the chapel continued to make its influence felt in subtle ways, and crowds often came to Rosslyn to wreak further damage in the name of their Protestant sensitivities in the face of anything that smacked to them of idolatry.

The chapel in disrepair

Thereafter, the chapel was somewhat neglected. The estate came into the possession of General James Sinclair, another member of the family, in 1736. He at least cared enough about the chapel to cause the windows to be glazed, the roof to be repaired and the floor to be relaid with flagstones, indicating, surely, that the chapel was being put to some sort of use, though what remains obscure. The Sinclairs were no longer laid to their long rest in the vaults under the chapel, as they had been until 1650.

When William Wordsworth and his sister, Dorothy, visited the chapel in the early autumn of 1807, it was already in danger of becoming a ruin. Dorothy recorded her impressions thus:

> Went to view the inside of the Chapel of Rosslyn, which is kept locked up, and so preserved from the injuries it might otherwise receive from idle boys; but as nothing is done to keep it together, it must, in the end, fall. The architecture within is exquisitely beautiful. The stone, both of the roof and walls, is sculptured with leaves and flowers, so delicately wrought that I could have admired them for hours, and the whole of their groundwork is stained by time, with the softest colours. Some of those leaves and flowers were tinged perfectly green, and at one part the effect was most exquisite — three or four leaves of a small fern, resembling that which we call Adder's Tongue, grew round a cluster of them at the top of a pillar, and the natural product and the artificial were so intermingled that, at first, it was not easy to distinguish the living plant from the other, they being of an equally determined green, though the fern was of a deeper shade.

The guide to the chapel in the time of the Wordsworths' visit was one Annie Wilson, described by a reporter from *The Gentleman's Magazine* of September 1817 — in decidedly ungentlemanly terms — as 'an old crone'. Annie was particularly keen to show visitors the Apprentice Pillar, designed, according to the legend, by the apprentice Tam Nimmo, from Orkney, who dreamed of the pillar, and drew what he had seen in his dream. This he showed to Earl William, who approved the design. Annie Wilson used to point out its features, and other aspects of the chapel, with a long divining rod:

> 'There ye see it, gentlemen, with the lace bands winding sae beautifully roond aboot it. The maister had gane awa to Rome to get a plan for it, and while he was awa his 'prentice made a plan himself and finished it. And when the maister cam back and fand the pillar finished, he was sae enraged that he took a hammer and killed the 'prentice. There you see the 'prentice's face — up there in ae corner, wi' a red gash in the brow, and his mother greeting for him in the corner opposite. And there in another corner, is the maister, as he lookit just before he was hanged; it's him wi' a kind o' ruff roond his face.'

An aspect of the story that she did not relate was that similar legends are told of Huish Episcopi in Somerset, of windows in Melrose Abbey, and of Lincoln and Rouen Cathedrals, which perhaps indicates that the truth is here disguised in a legend understood by those concerned in the building of Christian churches.

The chapel restored

Queen Victoria, visiting in 1842, also indicated her concern for the fabric of the building, and hoped that 'so unique a gem should be preserved to the country,' but it was in 1861, that Lady Helen Wedderburn of Rosebank, and the Rev R. Cole, the Military Chaplain of Greenlaw, had the inspiration, quite independently of each other, that the chapel should once again become a place of worship. The Third Earl of Rosslyn was so enthusiastic about this idea, that he put the matter into the hands of the prominent architect Sir David Bryce. Bryce gladly took up the work, and there was generous support from several interested parties. The work was thorough, and the chapel was rededicated in 1862.

Bryce, himself a Freemason, saw so much symbolism familiar to Freemasons in the chapel that he incorporated new carvings showing quasi-angelic beings in Masonic gestures along the east wall in the Lady Chapel. The great inspiration for both the Templars and the Freemasons is the Temple of Solomon. Certainly Solomon's Temple was an inspiration for the first builders of Rosslyn, and this is reflected in some of the chapel's original carvings.

Further work was undertaken by the Fourth Earl of Roslin, who added the baptistery with an organ loft above it in the years 1880–81. Rosslyn Chapel was now a fully functioning Episcopalian church. It was the Collegiate Church of Saint Matthew, once again, after a gap of two and a half centuries.

Rosslyn becomes famous

A century after its rededication, Trevor Ravenscroft, author of *The Spear of Destiny* and *The Cup of Destiny* became convinced that the chapel holds one of the great mysteries of medieval Christianity: the Holy Grail. The cup used by Christ at the Last Supper was, according to Ravenscroft, to be found within the Apprentice Pillar, encased in lead. Whatever was the process by which he arrived at this conclusion, he was certainly convinced of its truth, and campaigned to have the Pillar opened. This the chapel authorities, understandably, did not allow.

Other books were published that included the chapel in their preoccupations, among which was *Holy Blood and Holy Grail*, published in 1989. This work connected the Sinclair or Saint Clair family with the Priory of Sion, a shadowy institution whose task was or is, allegedly, to protect the secret of the bloodline of the Merovingian kings of France, who were displaced in the eighth century by the Carolingian kings. The 'secret' is that the Merovingians were descended from Jesus of Nazareth and Mary Magdalene, Jesus having escaped from Jerusalem before the Crucifixion, lived happily ever after in the South of France. The supposed connection of the Sinclair family with the Priory of Sion naturally involved Rosslyn Chapel, built by the Sinclairs. If this scenario seems familiar, it was used by Dan Brown in his *Da Vinci Code*. This was the book which, more than any, sparked an interest in Rosslyn Chapel unprecedented in its history. An enormous amount of tourists have come to measure their own responses against the imaginations of the place put forward in so many popular books, newspaper articles, TV documentaries and so on. Never before had Rosslyn evoked so much interest on so global a scale.

Two more discoveries have been made in the recent past. Stuart Mitchell, an Edinburgh composer, found that patterns on the cubic projections in the Lady Chapel have a close resemblance with Chladni patterns. These are patterns formed by powder or fine sand on a metal plate when a violin bow is drawn along its edge. Different plates may be tuned to certain musical tones, and these form distinct patterns. Mitchell took down these patterns from the carvings, worked out what tones they represent, and wrote a motet based on the tones, which he has scored for the instruments to be seen carved on to the capitals of the pillars in the chapel. The work, called *The Rosslyn Motet*, is available now on CD, and is a simple but strangely haunting piece of work. Interestingly, it contains the so-called 'Devil's chord', the augmented fourth, banned by the Catholic Church in religious music, as it sounded too disturbing. This chord opens the piece and appears again towards the middle.

The second recent discovery is of a small window, pentagonal in shape, and of red glass, that predates the rose window of 1844, and sits just above it. On Saint Matthew's Day, September 21, and on March 21, the sun's rays shine directly through the window, bringing a bright red light into the chapel. This window was rediscovered by Alan Butler and John Ritchie. They point out in their book *Rosslyn Revealed* that medieval churches were built to face the rising sun on the saint's day connected with the church. Saint Matthew's day is September 21, the autumn equinox. Rosslyn Chapel, being named for Saint Matthew, faces exactly due east, and hence receives the light of both the spring and autumn equinoxes. The small red window allows light to shine in to the chapel, as the equinoctial sun's rays fall parallel with it, forming a bright aura round the face of Christ in the window in the west wall opposite, though, when the chapel was first built, there was no window; just a blank wall, the better to reflect the light of the equinoctial sunrise. It seems that the complexity of the chapel's construction is still slowly being revealed and appreciated.

As I write, Rosslyn Chapel sits under a canopy, a construction like a Dutch barn, to shield it from the worst attacks of the weather, and to allow the structure to dry out enough so that the carvings can be preserved more effectively than previously possible. Although this free-standing structure is not particularly attractive, it allows visitors to climb up on to a catwalk from which the roof and outer structure of the chapel can be more closely seen, and you can admire the surrounding countryside, especially the beautiful Roslin Glen. Important restoration work is projected for the near future. This is made possible by the revenue generated by the many thousands of visitors to Rosslyn every year, for after nearly six hundred years, it still is a place of pilgrimage.

1. The Expulsion from Eden

On the back of the pillar immediately behind the High Altar, and facing east, is a carving, much damaged, of the expulsion from Paradise. The ancient legends, many of which were collected by Micha Joseph bin Gorion under the title Mimekor Yisrael, *tell us that there were worlds created by the gods before our world was created. 'Enoch,' says the old Hebrew story, 'had been exalted beyond others of his kind in the very first world that preceded the world of Adam.' In another of the old tales we are told that 'a thousand worlds the Lord had created at the beginning. Then He created still more worlds, and He continued to create and destroy worlds, until He created our world.'*

The Creation

The Bible tells us that Adam was made on the sixth 'day' of Creation. The first of these 'days' saw the forming of heaven and earth, but all in a chaos, 'without form and void'. The Elohim, or gods then said 'Let there be light,' and light and darkness became separated. The second day, or period of creation, saw the separation of the waters; those below and those above. On the third day, dry land appeared and the gathering of the waters below into the oceans of the world. The potential for plant life was given by the

Elohim in this day. Sun, moon and stars appeared on the fourth day, and on the fifth, the creatures of the seas were brought into being. On the sixth day, the land animals were made, and mankind was created, bearing the imprint of the gods as the one made with an element of the divine, creative imagination.

Next we learn an important thing: the human being was not yet of the earth, but a purely spiritual being, living in the imagination of the gods. He existed, but not yet as a physical being. The Bible tells us: 'Then the Lord God formed a man from the dust of the ground and breathed into his nostrils the breath of life. Thus the man became a living creature.' This only happened after the Six Days of Creation that we read about in *The Book of Genesis:* 'Then the Lord God planted a garden in Eden away to the east, and there he put the man whom he had formed.'

In this island of peace, this garden in the east, Adam, the human being formed of the substance of the earth, lived. The Archangel Michael came to him with the Book of Wisdom, which contained all the wisdom of creation, but this was a wisdom that did not touch Adam's innocence. This book he read until it became part of his nature, and he held it to his breast.

But now the time came that what was masculine in Adam should be separated from what was feminine. Adam was made to fall into a sleep. The angels who had worked on the form of Adam's body were then asked how they had done their work, and those who had made the ribs of Adam said: 'We have made bones that reach out and clasp in an embrace to protect and support the heart and the breath, for the breath and the blood are the source of life.'

Adam and Eve cast out of the Garden of Eden

Then said the Elohim: 'Then you shall make woman to be the protector and preserver of life.' Thus it was, and Eve was made by those angels who made the ribs, and upon the ribs of Eve they placed the organs of nutrition for the newborn, so that any child born to a woman would be held close to the heart, and hear its beating, and close to the breath, and feel its warmth, as they fed at the breast. To Eve was given the womb, and to Adam the seed.

Then Adam awoke, and beheld his wife, and the light of the gods veiled them in glory, though they could still behold each other.

Now the Devil, who had been a bright archangel in Heaven, had been angry at the creation of Adam, for it was said among the gods that this was one who would take his place with the highest gods at the end of time. He pondered how he could bring Adam and his wife Eve to their destruction. In the garden where the gods had placed them there grew two trees, the Tree of Life, and the Tree of the Knowledge of Good and Evil. The Lord God had forbidden Adam to eat of the fruit of these trees, though of all the rest of the trees he freely could eat the fruit. So the Devil entered into the body of a serpent, and tempted Adam to eat of the forbidden fruit, but Adam, remembering what he had been told by the gods, and what he had learned in the Book of Wisdom, refused to eat.

But Eve had not been made when the commandment was given. Now, some say that when the Devil came to her, she acted in ignorance of the commandment concerning the fruit of the forbidden trees, and that she sinned through the subtlety of the Devil's wiles and cunning. Others say that she indeed knew the commandments, but saw the strength and power of the Devil, and knew that he was mighty. Therefore, she decided that she would make a sacrifice that would prevent worse evil coming into the world, for if the Devil did indeed finally tempt Adam to eat of the fruit of the Tree of Life, then all would perish from the earth. But if they ate of the fruit of the Tree of Knowledge of Good and Evil, their life would become arduous, but life would not perish from the face of the earth. She also knew that if Adam ate of the fruit of this latter tree first, his thinking would be hard and cold, but if she ate of it first, this would happen only after long passages of time and only after many generations had come and gone in the world.

These are the stories of Eve's temptation. Whoever has the right of it; Eve ate of the fruit of the Tree of Knowledge of Good and Evil, and persuaded Adam to do the same. At once, the glory of holy light that veiled them faded away, and they appeared to each other as if naked. They found this nakedness shaming, and used leaves to cover themselves, and when they became aware of the presence in the garden of the gods, they strove to hide from them. The Lord God, seeing them in their nakedness, sent a high god, one of the Cherubim, to guard the gates of Paradise against them.

In the days of their innocence, Adam and Eve were given everything that they needed. Now, they had to provide for themselves through their labour. Children would be born to them, but not in innocence, and their birth would be travail. They also knew that in their bodies of flesh and blood they were not immortal, but that these bodies would die, and their substance return to the earth from which they were made. Adam took with him from Paradise the Book of Wisdom, and this was handed down from generation to generation.

Thus Adam and Eve were created in Paradise, and through the cunning of the Serpent they had to leave their paradisal beginnings. They began the work of the world, and their sons continued it.

It is said by some that before Adam awoke, the gods looked upon Eve and saw that she was beautiful, and some tell that they fathered upon her the first-born of the world, whose name was Cain. She herself said: 'I have gained a husband in the Lord' or, the Lord is now my husband. The worst effects of the expulsion from Paradise were not yet felt in the birth of Cain. We are told further, in the old legends that he was born without pain after a pregnancy without suffering, but this is not told in all the tales. We learn that Cain was the first child, and after him came Abel. Abel was a shepherd, and a warden of the creatures of creation, whereas Cain took what the world gave him, but changed it. He made tools to drive into the earth to plant vegetables. His name means 'Man of ability'. The gods were divided in their love for the sons of Adam, and some refused the offerings that Cain brought to the altar, and accepted the sacrifice of the lamb that Abel brought. Tension arose between the brothers, and Cain slew Abel because his offering was refused in favour of Abel's.

Thus, through Cain, the earth that had been virgin soil now lost that virginity, while the first spilling of blood upon the land was another loss of the earth's innocence. Cain had to bear the responsibility for this through cycles of time.

2. The Golden Legend

In Rosslyn Chapel stands the Apprentice Pillar, and all the vegetation carved within the chapel seems to grow like the branches and foliage of a tree, from this pillar. It stands in the south-east of the chapel, and is wound round with garlands. At its roots are dragons that constantly gnaw away at them, to show that all life is in balance. This pillar represents the Tree of Life when it had intertwined itself with the Tree of Knowledge, and it stands like an archetypal plant, the source of all plant growth, inside the chapel, where only the undersides of the leaves are shown, and outside it, where the carved leaves show their upper sides.

The Golden Legend

Adam, with the Garden of Eden now closed to him, came at last to the end of his days. As he lay dying, he sent his son Seth to the Gates of Eden to bring back some drops of the Oil of Mercy to anoint him for his passing.

Seth made his way through the hard and rocky terrain of the Land of Nod, and after a long and weary journey, he came in sight of the Gates of the Garden.

'What do you wish for, Son of Adam?' said a voice like a rushing wind.

'I seek the Oil of Mercy for my father who is sick unto death,' Seth replied, 'and so I come here to beg for it.'

'You know why your father may not approach these gates?' the voice asked.

'He ate of the fruit of the Tree of Knowledge of Good and Evil,' Seth answered, readily enough.

'Just so,' the angelic being replied, 'and know, Son of Adam, that the Tree of Knowledge of Good and Evil has grown so close to the Tree of Life that they wind round each other, and are as a single tree. Now, turn your back, for the Gates will be opened, and you may not see within the Garden.'

Seth turned his back, and after some little time had passed, he was bidden to turn round. At his feet lay a small cruse of the Oil of Mercy, and three seeds.

'My thanks for the oil,' said Seth, 'but what are these seeds?'

'These are three seeds from the Trees that now grow as one. You should place them beneath the tongue of your father Adam before you lay him in the earth on top of the hill that shall be shown to you.'

Seth returned and did as he was instructed, placing the seeds beneath Adam's tongue at his death, before he was lain in the ground at the top of the hill.

In time, the three seeds grew and wound round each other, making a single mighty tree.

Enoch, the son of Seth, took a branch from the tree and planted it, and the branch grew into another great tree. From this tree he cut a staff which in time passed to Noah, and it was in his hand as he supervised the construction of the great Ark that was to survive the Flood.

Once the flood waters had receded, and Noah was old and stricken in years, the staff was handed on to his son Shem. From Shem it passed to Abraham and it was inherited by Jacob.

When Jacob went to visit Joseph when he grew to power in Egypt, he took the staff with him, and presented it to him as a gift. Joseph kept it and honoured it until his death, but when he died, it was looted from his house.

After many generations had passed, it came into the hands of Jethro the Midianite. This was his priestly staff of office. Moses came to serve Jethro after his flight from Egypt, and after forty years had gone by, and Moses had served Jethro faithfully, Jethro gave the staff to Moses as symbol of his destiny when he should return to Egypt to bring the Children of Israel out of the Land of Goshen and the slavery that bound them.

Meanwhile, down all the days that passed, the tree of Enoch grew ever stronger, but far from the eyes and sight of men. But when Solomon ordered that his father's wish be fulfilled, and a temple built to house the Name of God and the Ark of His Covenant with men, the architect Hiram Abiff went looking for a suitable wood to be the pillar to support the structure. To him was granted a sight of the tree, and he knew that this was a tree of special virtue and strength. He caused to be cut from it a great beam that was to become the central supporting pillar, and thus it was done. But when they came to place the pillar within the structure, it would not go through the doorway. This was a great puzzle to Hiram, and he measured the length and the width and the breadth, and measured these against the size of the doorway, and there was no reason that he could see why the beam should not pass through the doorway, and yet, try as they might, nothing availed, and the beam would not pass through. Therefore Hiram ordered that the beam should be placed over the river as part of the bridge that connected the northern banks with the southern banks.

Now, Balchis, the Queen of Sheba, came to meet Solomon, and to marvel at the great temple that was now becoming famous in all the lands round about.

The capital of the Apprentice Pillar, showing Green Men, Angels with musical instruments, an Angel with an open book, and vegetation branching out across the chapel.

But when she came to the river, she saw the great beam that was part of the bridge, and she stopped and worshipped. When she was asked why she showed such reverence to a piece of wood, she told them that it was on wood from the same tree as this beam that the Saviour of all the world should hang.

The generations from Solomon to the birth of Jesus were twenty-eight, and the tree grew stronger through all this time, but few were they who saw it. But when the judgment was made that He should be crucified, it was from this tree that the wood for the Cross was cut.

Now the cross that the Romans used to hang those judged guilty had a stem that reached down into the ground, like a tree, and two arms that stretched out on either side, parallel with the backbones of the beasts of the field, while the centre piece pointed to the skies. But the carpenters who fashioned the cross for Jesus Christ found that the shape of the wood, and the knots in it, meant that the two cross-pieces did not reach out horizontally, but were raised, like arms raised in prayer or supplication. They showed this to the officer of the soldiers, but he said: 'Let it stand thus,' and so it was that this cross was different from the others. In this way, the prophecy of the Queen of Sheba came to pass.

3. The Green Men — Osiris

Visitors to Rosslyn soon have their attention drawn to the multitude of 'Green Men', faces that appear out of the carved foliage that appears in profusion in the chapel. Rosslyn is not alone in having Green Men appearing among the decoration, but it is entirely alone in the amount of them. There are well over a hundred of these small faces, appearing throughout the chapel, inside and out, and another, more surprising phenomenon is that, as you follow them round the chapel in a clockwise direction, they grow older, and the last one on the path has a face touched by death, skull-like and hollow-eyed. This aging has been noticed by Mark Oxbrow and Ian Robertson in their book Rosslyn and the Grail. *What is depicted here is the rhythm of the year. Nature is youthful in the springtime and grows towards the 'death' of winter, after which it is reborn. The Green Men faces personify the world of Nature in its yearly rhythm of death and rebirth.*

In pre-Christian times this annual rhythm was seen as an earthly reflection, within time, of events in the heavens among the gods, in eternity. Gods whose death and rebirth were celebrated within the world of Nature included Baldur among the Northern European people, Adonis in the Greek world, Tammuz further east among the Phoenician peoples; but the origin and archetype of them all was Osiris, chief of the Gods of Egypt, after Ra, the Creator. William Sinclair knew that he could not place a clear representation of what would have been judged to be a pagan deity into what was to be a place of Christian worship. Nevertheless, Osiris is the origin and archetype of the Green Men.

The youngest of the 'Green Man' faces: nineteenth century replacement of a damaged original.

The skull-like green man face, centre, on the capital of the Journeyman's Pillar.

The story of Osiris

The first and greatest of the gods was Ra, born of the immense and chaotic abyss Nuu. Ra thought, and his thinking was creation. He created all things from his thinking. Earth and sky were separated from one another by the thinking of Ra, and the earth was Qeb, the Father, and sky was called Nut, the Mother. The Upper Air was called Shu and the Lower Air was called Tefenet.

From Qeb and Nut was born earthly creation, through the thinking of Ra. Osiris was the first-born of these gods, and when he was born, a voice rang through the heavens and the earth, crying: 'Behold! Now is born the Lord of all things!'

After Osiris came Isis, who was his sister and wife, and Thoth the Wise One. The sister of Isis was Nephthys. Last of these was Typhon-Set, whose birth rent a hole in his mother's side, for he came raging into the world.

When Osiris reigned, there was peace in the world. Weapons were unknown in the hands of men. The speech of men and women was sweet and wholesome, and music was heard throughout the world. It was Osiris who taught the secrets of the growth of the soil to men, so that the crops could grow and feed the people, and wine be made of the grapes. All was green and abundant where Osiris reigned, and all was harmonious between men and women, and the pattern of their harmony was Osiris and Isis, the King and the Queen of all created things.

But Typhon-Set dwelled in the waste places, where no green thing grew. His was the desert and all therein, and he hated the growth of the soil. All that Osiris had taught to men was hateful to Typhon-Set, and he laid plans against the life of Osiris, but Isis was watchful and baffled his plans at every turn.

The larnax of Typhon-Set

Typhon-Set became more cunning. He gazed at Osiris from far off, and he looked at his shadow. From the shadow of Osiris he noted the proportions of his body and kept them in his heart, and from the measurements of the body of Osiris he constructed a larnax, which is a chest made to the size and shape of a person.

The time was approaching when the waters would recede, and Typhon-Set invited everyone to a feast before the time of the drought began. All the children of Qeb and Nut were called to the feast. Thoth and Nephthys, the wife of Typhon-Set came, and Isis came and Osiris. As they enjoyed the feast, they could see in plain view the larnax that Typhon-Set had made so cunningly from the wood of many a fragrant and aromatic tree. This larnax drew the admiration of those at the feast, and Typhon-Set said that he would give it to whoever could fit inside it exactly. Typhon-Set himself lay in it, but its proportions were not right for him. Nephthys laid herself in it, but she was not the right shape for it. Thoth tried, and he too was not the right shape to fit the larnax, and neither was Isis, when she tried.

Now it was the turn of Osiris, and he laid aside his crown and lowered himself into the larnax. The form of his body filled the length of it, and the breadth of it so perfectly, and his countenance shone nobly within it, and the perfection of his body was fair to be seen within it, and all who stood by were astonished and praised the beauty of Osiris and the workmanship of Typhon-Set, but Typhon-Set stood apart, and called to his men.

At once, six dozen of the attendants of Typhon-Set rushed into the room and put a heavy cover on the larnax. Some kept the other children of Qeb and Nut at a distance while others drove nails through the cover into the larnax, and sealed it with lead. Isis and Thoth and Nephthys could do nothing against the strength of the attendants, and could do no more than to run, following those who bore the larnax through the night to the banks of the river, but in the darkness they lost each other.

In the light of the dawn, Isis, Thoth and Nephthys found each other again, and they followed the spoor of the men who had carried away the body of Osiris in the larnax. But the larnax had been thrown into the river, and now was borne away to the sea.

The wanderings of Isis

Isis followed the bank of the river until she came to the sea, but she did not know where the sea had taken Osiris. She crossed the sea and asked wherever she could about the larnax, but none could help her, though little children followed her and tried to help her in her misery.

Now the larnax had been washed ashore in a great wave in the land of Byblos, and it had lain in a thicket of trees. One of these trees had lifted the larnax as it grew, and wrapped it around with its branches, and spread its bark around it, until the larnax was part of the growing tree, and spread the fragrance of its many aromatic woods to the tree.

The king and queen of Byblos were called Melqart and Astarte. They were told of this tree whose fragrance was so wonderful, and King Melqart sent men to cut down the tree, to trim away the branches and to bring it to him, so that it could stand as a pillar in his house. This was done, and the tree stood as a pillar in the palace of Melqart and Astarte, and they wound garlands round it.

The news of the woman who sat by the grove of trees came to the ears of the queen Astarte, and she came to see for herself. When Astarte approached, Isis arose and stretched out her hand and placed it in blessing on Astarte's head. Astarte felt herself filled with a wonderful fragrance. Astarte asked if Isis would come to the palace and be the nursemaid to her child, and Isis agreed.

Isis nursed the princeling in the hall where the pillar stood, wound round with garlands. She put her finger in the child's mouth, and this nourished the child. At night she stripped away the wood from the pillar and threw the wood on the fire. In this fire she would lay the princeling, who would take no hurt from the flames, but lie among them as they burned softly round him. Isis would then take the form of a swallow, and fly round the pillar, singing a song of lamentation.

One night, Astarte entered the hall, and saw her son lying among the flames, and snatched him out with a loud cry of distress. Isis, in the form of a swallow, called to Astarte from the pillar, and said: 'Foolish and sudden! Hadst thou suffered the child to lie another night and yet one more night in the fire of the wood of this pillar, he would have gained immortality! Now, though his life shall be long, he shall not be immortal.'

Astarte drew back in astonishment. 'Who, then, are you, who say such things?' she demanded.

'I am Isis, and within this pillar is entombed Osiris my consort. We are the children of Qeb and of Nut, and I have long sought my husband before I found him within your palace, closed up in this pillar.'

Melqart, when he heard this, gave orders for the pillar to be taken down and cloven open. There was the larnax in which lay Osiris. Isis wrapped the larnax in linen, and it was borne out of the palace and set upon a ship. The ship sailed back to Egypt, and Isis stirred not at all from beside the larnax.

The return of Isis and Osiris

In Egypt, Isis took the body of Osiris out of the larnax, and she breathed her own breath into him, and though in her own form, let her swallow's wings grow broad and wide upon her back to waft the breath of life into Osiris. Osiris awoke, and he and Isis dwelled far away from the children of Qeb and Nut.

Now Typhon-Set loved to hunt the gazelle whose beauty and grace offended him, and one night he was out hunting, and he discovered Isis and Osiris sleeping peacefully in the moonlight. In a rage, he fell upon the sleeping Osiris, and tore him into fourteen pieces. These he scattered about the land, and death fell upon the soil of Egypt for the first time. Men began to take up weapons and to make war; speech between men and women lost its sweetness and the music was stilled. The green growth of the soil grew less and less, and the desert waste began to spread. Thoth and Nephthys were afraid as they stood before Typhon-Set, and all that Ra had brought into being through his thought was in danger of destruction.

Isis travelled through the marshes in a boat made of reeds, with Nephthys at her side, and together they gathered the pieces of the body of Osiris. One after another, each one was found. On an island floating among the reeds of the marshes, she put the pieces together, and sang over them, and breathed the breath of her body into the reformed body of Osiris, and peace began to come once again among warring men; music was heard once more. The growth of the soil began again in all its fullness.

A voice came to Isis to tell her that Osiris lived again indeed, but now he lived in the Underworld, where he was the judge of the dead, and through his justice men and women were immortal.

A child was born to Isis, whose name was Horus, and Thoth and Nephthys kept him safe on the floating island of Chemmis. Horus would one day be king and would strive against the power of Typhon-Set, though Isis would not have her brother slain, and made him live among the lesser gods where his power was reduced for ever.

4. Hermes Trismegistus

In the Lady Chapel at the east of Rosslyn, close to the stairs that lead to the Lower Chapel, is a face that at first seems to belong to the many Green Men that are to be seen all over the chapel, inside and out. But this is larger than the others, and the features are clearly defined, youthful and slightly feminine. This face is traditionally associated in Rosslyn mythology with Hermes Trismegistus, the Thrice-Great Hermes whose teachings were known to Plato and the Ancients. In common with the Green Men, foliage sprouts from the mouth, but does not link up with the carved plant-life that is so luxuriant in the chapel, as it does with the rest of the Green Men. In fact, it suggests a threefold crown, or diadem. The mouth and jaw symbolize here the will, as the nose and central plane of the face is connected with the feelings and the brow with thinking. The face of Hermes shows what is achieved through the transformation through the will of those aspects of the human being that in Indian terminology are called Manas, *or transformed soul;* Bodhi, *the life force transformed into a higher quality; and finally* Atman, *the physical nature of the human being itself raised to a new level of existence. But the appearance of Hermes Trismegistus in Rosslyn indicates an important link with the oldest mysteries of mankind, and in particular, of Ancient Egypt.*

William Sinclair and his colleague in the design and building of Rosslyn, Gilbert Haye, were practised esotericists, well aware of the importance and influence of Hermes. Indeed, at the time of the building of Rosslyn, considerable importance was attached to writings attributed to Hermes, even though doubts were later expressed about their authenticity. Still, the so-called Hermetica current in the fifteenth century reflected with a high degree of accuracy the teachings of the original Hermes. The rituals of the Hermetic initiation of Egypt were reborn in a new way in the initiations of Craft Masonry; in a different way in the Templar rituals and later, in the practices of the Rosicrucian Brotherhood. The story of that initiation into the secrets of Hermes belongs here.

The 'original Hermes': this begs a question. The name Hermes in the sense that it appears here is not the name of a single individual, but rather, a title. One who had attained the very highest initiation into the mysteries of Ancient Egypt could call himself Hermes, or to use the Egyptian name, Thoth. There were very few who reached such a level of initiation.

The face of Hermes Trismegistus.

The Isis initiation

Thousands of years before Christ, Egypt reached its greatness. Asclepius, a young student of the mysteries, looking around at the marvels of Egyptian architecture and art, was told by Hermes-Thoth: 'O Egypt, Egypt! For future generations, nothing will remain of thee but unbelievable tales and words carved in stone!' In those days, water lapped around the base of the Sphinx, the early representation of the terrestrial Isis. The culture of the god Ammon-Ra flourished in those early years, until the great invasions of the Hyksos, the so-called Shepherd-Princes, an Asiatic people who overran most of Egypt, and drove the keepers of the mysteries underground. Indeed, the Hyksos made a great contribution to the cultural and economic life of Egypt during the nine hundred years of their rule, but once they were overthrown, the ancient mysteries that had been kept hidden were unchanged. Men had come to learn them, and if successful, to maintain them, from those schools that were the preparatory colleges for the greater mysteries.

The student of the mysteries needed more than an overwhelming thirst for knowledge if he were to become successful. He who put himself into the hands of Hermes Trismegistus needed courage and steadfastness. He would already have known something of *The Book of the Dead,* and the voyage of the immortal part of the human being after death; the review of one's life, the region of fire, burning away the imperfections gathered in life; the purification of the astral body or soul; the meeting with two pilots, the good pilot who looks forward and the evil pilot whose face is turned to the side; the trial before the forty two judges of earthly life and the defence conducted by the god Thoth. If at the end of this journey the weight of the soul was in balance in the scales with the ostrich feather of Isis, then it would be admitted into the light of Osiris. But were things really as was described in *The Book of the Dead?* 'Isis and Osiris know!' was all the answer the novice received, and the names were not spoken aloud but whispered.

Knowing the contents of *The Book of the Dead* had a profound effect on some of those familiar with it. Those who wished to penetrate the mysteries to their very depths would eat no meat or fish, and remain chaste. A revolution in the moral life was necessary if one was to undertake such a path of enlightenment. The French esotericist and researcher Édouard Schuré described fully the path of the postulant in his book *The Great Initiates*.

The novice would arrive at the great Temple of Osiris at Thebes, and be led by servants to an inner court. There, the hierophant would welcome him, and ask him about his family, where he had come from and where his studies so far had been conducted, and who had taught him. So deep and piercing was the gaze of the hierophant that the novice, or postulant, would feel it going through him searchingly, reading the deepest secrets of his being. If the postulant were found wanting, the hierophant would simply point to the door, and the interview would be concluded, and any hope of his learning the secrets of the temple was dashed. If he were successful, he would be led through the temple precincts to a statue of Isis, life size, and veiled, with the inscription beneath: 'No mortal has lifted my veil.'

Behind the statue was a door, flanked by two columns; one red, the other black. The red column signified the ascent to the light of Osiris, but the other indicated the death and annihilation of the human spirit in matter.

'Here you stand at the portal. To go through this door means madness to the weak, and death for the wicked. Only those whose strength of purpose is allied to good will may find life beyond this threshold. Think: have you the courage? Have you the purity of soul? If there is any doubt in your mind, go back now. Once this door closes behind you, there is no return.'

Thus the hierophant addressed the novice, and it was a brave man indeed who would dare to take the next step, through the gateway to initiation. But more preparation was necessary before the door would be opened to him. If he was still wishing to take the lonely step through the portal, he would be taken back through the temple complex and required to join the servants, with whom he would spend a week, working diligently and speaking to no-one. Silence was an absolute demand of the postulant, as he performed the most mundane and dirty of tasks, his only connection to those mysteries that he wished to master was the music of the holy psalms, borne on the warm air to him in the midst of his drudgery.

At last the evening arrived when he would face his greatest ordeal. Two acolytes led him back to the door behind the statue of Isis. Here was a long, dark corridor, with no visible way out, and shadowy forms on either side of the dim passageway of human bodies with animal heads, large and forbidding in the darkness, each one appearing to watch his every step in silent mockery at his presumption.

At the end of the corridor were two more silent figures, one a mummy, the other a human skeleton. Between these two was a hole. The two acolytes bade farewell to the novice here.

'You can still turn back,' one of the acolytes said. The other added: 'There is still time.'

But the novice had come so far. Fear and the dedication to know the truth wrestled within him. At last, he knew that to turn back now was a defeat that would weigh heavily on him for the rest of his life.

'I shall go forward,' he said.

The acolytes took their leave. They closed the door of the entrance with a loud bang that echoed through the passage and smote the novice's heart. He had now to crawl on hands and knees through a low, downward-sloping passage with nothing more to light his path than the flickering naphtha lamp in his left hand, and that hardly illuminated anything, but rather seemed to allow shapes to loom up from the darkness. Voices resonated through the darkness, repeating the same warning: 'They perish here that lust for knowledge and power.'

The passage grew wider, but sloped more steeply downwards until he came to a shaft that fell before him into blackness. In the sputtering light of his naphtha lamp, he could make out the rung of a ladder down into the abyss. No other way presented itself to him. Slowly he made his way down, trying not to drop his lamp as he held on to the rungs.

The darkness below him was profound. He could see nothing in those depths. His foot reached down for the next rung, but — there was none! The ladder finished here, but the abyss went on seemingly for ever into the blackness. What could he do? There was no way back. What was demanded of him now? Was this the end of his search, alone in this subterranean darkness? With an effort, he moved his lamp to this right hand as he looked around in the gloom. Here, to his right was a crevice. If he was careful, he could make his way from the ladder into it.

He managed to manoeuvre his way from the metal rungs into the crevice, and now his lamp showed him a flight of steps; a spiral staircase cut into the living rock. He began to climb, every step taking him away from that dreadful abyss.

At last he stood before a grating of bronze, and beyond it was a great, well-lit hall, with pictures or scenes painted on the walls in two groups of eleven.

A priest, new to the novice, opened the grating, and led him into the hall.

'Well done, my son. You have passed the first test,' said the priest, and led him past the frescoes, stopping at each one to explain its meaning. Each one was associated with a letter and a number, and each picture had a triple meaning: one that had its echoes in the divine world; one that referred to the world of the human spirit, or intellect; and one that was to be understood with reference to the world of nature, the physical world. Thus, the keys to understanding at this level of initiation were threefold. The first of these was the Magus in a white robe of purity and golden crown of light, with the sceptre of authority in his hand. He symbolized in the divine realm, Absolute Being from which all creation flows; in the realm of the spirit, the original unity, the synthesis of all numbers; in the world of nature, the human being who alone among created beings in the world can will his evolution as a being of spirit. This and the other twenty-one pictures constituted the first book of the teachings of Hermes-Thoth. Gradually, the novice came to understand the meanings of them all; Isis of the Heavens, the Tower struck by lightning, the Chariot of Osiris, the Star; all the way to the Crown of the Illuminated Ones.

'This crown must be well understood,' the priest said. 'Those who are able to join their will to the Divine in the furtherance of Truth, Justice and Harmony after life in the world of Nature have the reward of free spirits; to enter into the realm of those who participate with the gods in guiding the forces of creation.'

The novice listened to these words with a mixture of awe and reverence. Something was beginning to dawn in his understanding of the meaning and purpose of human life on Earth. It opened up before him in a mighty picture, whose meaning was love.

But now the time came for further trials. The priest led the novice to a door and opened it. At the end of a corridor was a flaming furnace.

'If you are of good courage,' said the priest, 'the flames of the fire will be for you no more than the rose flowers in a garden.'

Borne up by the vision of love that the novice had received, he went forward. 'If I am unworthy,' he thought, 'let me be consumed by the flames indeed.'

The door closed behind him, and he approached the fire. But it was no more than the appearance of fire, made by daylight falling through sheets of wood cut into diamond shapes on an iron framework, and so thin as to allow the passage of light through them, colouring the light with fiery hues.

Illusion though it was, the effect on the novice was profound. He hurried through the path of fire, and came at once to a pool of stagnant water, in a chamber as dark as the previous one had been bright. The flames behind him cast eerie reflections on the blackness of the water. He waded in, the cold water becoming deeper and deeper, until at last he reached the far side.

Gasping and fearful, he was pulled out of the chill water by two acolytes who dried him and anointed him with sweet-smelling unguents, and told him to wait. The chamber was dim, lit by a bronze lantern. He waited, resting on a couch, and the tenth picture from the Book of Hermes-Thoth came into his mind; a wheel placed between two columns, upon which, on one side, was Anubis, spirit of good, and on the other, Set, the evil one, falling head downwards towards the abyss. Above the two sat the Sphinx, holding a sword. But what had this image to do with the place where he now found himself?

All at once, he heard the strains of melancholy music of harp and flute. And then, coming towards him, he saw a woman. She was tall and graceful, an Ethiopian beauty, all in diaphanous dress of red. He rose to meet her. She held in her left hand a cup, which she offered him. As she offered it, she smiled, and he realized that she was offering herself with the wine. This beautiful woman would be a fitting reward indeed for all that he had gone through. Her lips parted in a fresh smile as she offered him once more the cup. Her eyes were luminous in the shadowy chamber. Desire arose in him like flames. He formed the thought: 'I am on fire with desire.' And the memory of what he had just been through came back to him. She sat on the couch and raised the wine cup again, her right hand smoothing down her dress over her breast and belly, as if in invitation. He found himself moving towards the couch, but once again, the image of the Wheel arose in his mind's eye, and Set on the left hand, chained forever to the abyss.

He approached her, and reached for the cup. Taking it from her, he overturned it, letting the perfumed wine spill over the floor.

'The bliss of the body is the darkness of the soul,' he said, and turned away from her. She rose and left the chamber, and no sooner had she left than twelve acolytes entered, bearing torches. They led him to the sanctuary of the Temple, where the initiated priests of Osiris welcomed him. Before him in the sanctuary was a large statue of Isis, draped in velvet, a golden rose at her breast, and in her arms the child Horus. There, before the image of Isis and Horus, he was bound to silence by the most stringent of oaths. He had succeeded in the next trial. Had he submitted to the desires of the flesh, he would have been a slave to the temple for life. Any attempt to escape would have meant death.

Even now, though no longer a novice, he stood only at the threshold of knowledge. His studies began into the world of nature, the physical laws of the world. His 'teachers' hardly spoke to him, answering his questions sometimes with what seemed a brusque indifference, sometimes with the injunction: 'Be patient. Work.' Doubt began to torment him. He felt as though he was in a desert, with no-one to help him to slake his thirst.

In calmer moments he realized that the trials he had undergone were a foretaste of what he was experiencing now. His bodily desires were still strongly burning within him. The extent of his ignorance was greater than the dark abyss that he had escaped. The cold water was less of a torment than the doubts that assaulted him. If he could meet those trials then, could he not overcome the trials that his own nature set before him now?

Nevertheless, he still had moments when he despaired of ever learning anything of the knowledge that Hermes-Thoth possessed. His teachers remained distant.

'Who knows if you will ever be permitted to see the light of Osiris? It depends on you. Perhaps one day the lotus will rise from the depths of the pool; perhaps never in this lifetime. Be patient. Do your work diligently.'

With the passage of years, the postulant felt changes take place within him. The desires of his bodily nature burned less fiercely, and impatience and doubt gave way to a reverence for nature and the spirit. This grew into a deep piety which was noticed by the initiated priests, and one day, he was approached by the hierophant, the chief priest of the temple, he who led the postulant forward for the higher initiation.

'The time has come, my son,' said the hierophant. 'Through the purity of your heart, your power of self-denial and your love of truth, you have gained the right to be one among the company of the initiated.'

The brotherhood of the initiated accompanied the postulant to the lower crypt of the temple. There lay a cold stone sarcophagus into which the postulant climbed. He lay as one dead, and the cold began to spread through his body. He began to lose consciousness as the hymn for the dead, sung by the priesthood, echoed in that subterranean chamber.

'None escapes death. All living souls are destined for resurrection. He who goes into the tomb alive may enter the light of Osiris. As you lie here, wait for the light. You shall go through the gates of fear, and you shall attain to the mastery.'

Thus spoke the hierophant as the postulant felt pain like the death agony take hold of him. The priests filed out, and the singing rose in volume. They left behind them a lamp that gradually flickered and went out.

Now the postulant saw his life pass before him as in a great tableau. Everything he had ever done, everything that he had thought was plainly to be seen in this great picture. What had taken place in time now appeared in space. His consciousness became less and less distinct, as though borne away on a stream of time…

The last thing he recalled was the appearance of Isis, as she was depicted in the sanctuary, but younger, though still veiled. She carried in her hand a papyrus in which was the scroll of his life, his past lives, though pages were left blank for future lives.

'There shall come a time,' she said, 'when I shall unfold all before you. But for the time being, know me now as the sister of your soul. I shall come when you call upon me.'

Now, with a pain like birth, he found himself wrenched back into his temporal being, lying in the cold sarcophagus. He lay in his body, unable to move a finger, seized by a deathly lethargy, able only to open his eyes. There before him was the hierophant.

'You live again, one initiated in the light of Osiris,' he said, and the priests helped him out of the stone coffin. They gave him a cup of cordial to help him revive, as he felt life coursing through his veins again.

'Tell us of your journey,' said the hierophant. Most of what was revealed to the pupil of the Thrice-Great Hermes remains a deep secret, and we must leave it so.

†

Such was the initiation into the light of Osiris in the great days of Egypt, but a time came when those who entered the temple sleep in the cold, marble sarcophagus had a different story to tell, and it was indeed a sad and terrible report they made. Schuré makes no mention of this, but it is a phenomenon well-known to esoteric researchers, and an important aspect of many of the tales of Rosslyn. Those following the leadership of Hermes made a terrible discovery: Isis appeared to the initiated one in the mourning robes of a widow.

Osiris, the God who was her consort; He who was tricked into lying in the sarcophagus that his dark brother Typhon-Set had prepared and cast into the waters of the Nile; He whose remains Isis gathered together so that He might be reborn: Osiris was no longer reborn! Isis was a widow indeed. A light had been extinguished in the heavens. Those who had this grim experience of what seemed a catastrophe in the spiritual world were henceforth to be known as 'The Sons of the Widow' for many long centuries to come.

Hiram Abiff, architect of Solomon's Temple was called a Son of the Widow. Mani, the great spiritual leader of the third century ad was another, and so were those who followed him: the Cathars, the Bogomils, the Patarenes, the Albigensians. The Templars were also known as Sons of the Widow, as well as those who followed Craft Masonry. Those who conceived of and built Rosslyn were also of this brotherhood, and many symbols of this are to be found in the chapel, as we shall see. But this was the grim message of those who had been prepared in the mysteries of Hermes: Isis was a widow.

5. Melchizedek, Abraham and Isaac

A much damaged carving of Abraham, Isaac and the ram of sacrifice sits at the top of a capital close to an architrave that contains the words of Zerubabel, to which we shall return. On the other side of the aisle, there is a window, with the Kings of Israel carved around it, and within that framework of the Kings, ears of corn are shown, representing bread. At the bottom of the window, in the left corner is the carving of a bearded man holding a wine cup. This is Melchizedek, one of the most enigmatic figures of the Old Testament. Here is an account of the legend that brings these individuals together.

The birth and youth of Abram

There lived in Babylon a man named Terah, who had three sons, called Abram, which means 'Father of the Height', Nahor and Haran. This was in the days when Nimrod, the builder of great towers, was King of Babylon, also known as Chaldea. The legend tells that a new star shone in the heavens at the birth of Abram, and the room where the child was born was filled with light. Nimrod asked his priests about the new star, and was told that it signified the birth of one who would be a great leader. Nimrod then brought about a great massacre of new-born children and their mothers, imprisoning them in a temple before setting fire to it. Abram was taken away and hidden in a cave to escape this fate, and he remained there for a long time. During this period, he spent time with the priests of the Most High God, El-Elyon, God of Noah. To this priesthood of the Most High belonged Melchizedek. This was a priesthood that began with Noah's son Shem (who gives his name to the Semitic peoples) and maintained itself in secret, only appearing to affect human destinies at certain moments in history. The name Noah means 'a place of rest'. His other name was Menachem, 'the comforter'. These qualities of rest, peace and comfort are the heritage received by Melchizedek from the priests of Shem.

At last Abram left the Shem priests and returned to his father Terah in Babylon. Terah received him with great joy, and had chosen a wife for his son. This was Sarai, whose name means 'she who is destined to rule'. She was a woman of great beauty, and Abram was glad to receive her at his father's hand.

Nimrod the king at this time was building great towers reaching up to the heavens, and Abram could see that this showed a destructive pride. He debated with the priests of the genii of fire when they asked him why he did not pay homage to the god of fire. Abram replied that water puts out fire. They told him that they prayed to water, too, but Abram answered that clouds carry water.

'We also honour the clouds,' the priests said, but Abram replied: 'The winds scatter the clouds.' The priests said that the winds, too were their gods, and Abram's reply was that the earth is stronger than the wind. The priests grew angry, and wished to put Abram through the baptism of fire, but it had no effect on Abram; he remained unconvinced. He already had an intuition of the God beyond the spirits of the four elements, and this God he called Lord. Thus he prepared to leave Babylon and the city of Ur of the Chaldees.

It was a mighty caravan of travellers that left Ur of the Chaldees, for Abram was a man of princely bearing, and had a large household. He was joined by his nephew, Lot. Together they travelled to the land of Canaan, where Abram raised up an altar to his God.

Now, a famine fell upon the land, and Abram decided to journey to Egypt, though he knew that his wife Sarai would be seen as very comely by the Egyptians, and he knew that there was a danger that they would take her and kill him. Therefore he told Sarai to pose as his sister. Sure enough, when this rich caravan arrived in Egypt, Sarai's beauty was praised to Pharaoh, and he took her into his household, but laid no rough hand on Abram, whose faith was such that he had no fear for the well-being of his wife.

It followed that diseases and plagues struck Pharaoh's household, and when he consulted his wise men and soothsayers about the reason for their suffering, their magical researches told them that the cause was Sarai: she was another man's wife.

Pharaoh, not wishing to draw more trouble on his household, sent Sarai back to Abram, along with livestock, such as sheep, asses and camels. He also gave him slaves, both male and female, and Abram departed for Canaan, richer than when he had arrived.

Abram and Lot now parted company, and Lot went to make his home on what were then the lush and verdant plains of Jordan, near the city of Sodom. Abram remained in Canaan, and was honoured as a king and revered as a priest. He travelled through Canaan, and his God told him that his descendants would be as numerous as the dust, though as yet, Sarai had borne him no children.

There came a time of war among the kings of the region. Lesser kings rose up in rebellion against Kedorlaomer, King of Elam, but Abram remained apart from the strife, until he learned that his nephew Lot and all his household had been carried off by the men of Kedorlaomer. Abram was living by the terebinth groves belonging to his friend Mamre, at the time. On receiving the news, he gathered an army of three hundred and eighteen men and rode in pursuit, catching up with them just north of Damascus. He brought back the members of his family and their households, as well as the captured goods, flocks and slaves.

Abram and Melchizedek

On his triumphal return, he was met in the Valley of the Kings by Melchizedek, priest of the Most High God, who received Abram with bread and wine, and blessed him in the name of the Most High. Melchizedek saw in Abram one who was to be a servant of El-Elyon, the Most High God, though he worshipped Jahweh, but Jahweh reflected El-Elyon as the moon reflects the sunlight. The place where Melchizedek met Abram with bread and wine was later to be the place where Christ celebrated the sharing of bread and wine with His disciples at the Last Supper. But the city of Jerusalem was not yet built. Melchizedek lived in a place made holy when the great flood of Noah retreated.

An ancient legend tells that once Adam and Eve had been driven out of Paradise, Adam wished to consummate his marriage to her. Therefore he took gold, frankincense and myrrh and brought them to a cave where they could be together in memory of Paradise, and the cave was called the Treasure Cave. When Adam died, long years later, Noah was instructed by El-Elyon the Most High to take the body of Adam from the Treasure Cave where it had been lain, and place it in the Ark, and to place the gold, frankincense and myrrh on the coffin. When the waters receded, Noah and his son Shem went to a hill at the deepest part of the world, where the earth opened in a crevice in the form of a cross, to receive the body of Adam. This was where the body was laid to rest, and it was called the Hill of Golgotha. This was nearby the place where Melchizedek lived, out of the way of men. Now, he and Abram communed together on matters of a high spiritual nature, as priest to priest, and Abram gave to Melchizedek a tenth of the livestock that he had rescued, though this was to be a place where no blood was to be shed in sacrifice; only the sharing of bread and wine was to be the sacrament here, for it was a place of great holiness.

Abram becomes Abraham

When Abram left Melchizedek, he met Bera, the King of Sodom, who had been chased by Kedorlaomer into the tar pits of Siddim. Now that Kedorlaomer was defeated, he demanded from Abram the slaves and servants who had been rescued from the battle near Damascus, offering him wealth in exchange. But Abram despised the black magical practices of Sodom, and would have nothing to do with Bera, dividing the wealth he had won instead among Mamre and his brothers.

Now Sarai had still not given Abram a son, even though God had promised him that his descendants would be as numerous as the dust of the earth and the stars of the sky. So Sarai sent her Egyptian slave Hagar to Abram, and she conceived a son. When Hagar knew that she was pregnant, she began to feel superior to Sarai, and sneered and mocked her. Sarai complained of this to Abram, who told her to deal with Hagar as she wished. Sarai punished Hagar for her impertinence, and Hagar, unable to bear the punishment, ran away.

As she was resting by a well, an angel told her to return to Sarai, and told her a little of her son's destiny. Hagar could hardly believe that an angel had spoken to her in this remote place. 'Can I see a god and live?' she wondered. Thereafter, the well was called Beer-lahai-roi, which means the Well of One Who Has Seen a Vision and Lived. Hagar returned to the tents of Abram, and brought forth her son, who was named Ishmael.

One day, Abram felt himself in the presence of the Lord, and threw himself on the ground in reverence. He learned that the covenant was soon to be fulfilled, and Sarai would soon bring forth a son. Furthermore, he was no longer to be called Abram, Father of the Height, but Abraham, Father of a Host of Nations. Sarai, too, was to change her name. No longer was she to be named She who is Destined to Rule, but Sarah; She who is Consecrated to Rule. The boy that she was to bear would be called Isaac.

Not long after this, three men passed by Abraham's tents at his camp among the groves of terebinths. One was dressed all in white, one all in red, and the last all in green. These were no ordinary men, for an archangel spoke through each one. Michael spoke through the man all in white, Gabriel through the man in red and Raphael through the man in green. Abraham invited them to join him and eat. He washed their feet, in the tradition of those who welcome strangers in the desert lands, and they sat down together to eat. The man all in white asked where Sarah was.

'There in the tent,' replied Abraham.

'When I pass this way in a year's time, she shall have a son,' the stranger said. Sarah heard him and laughed. The man asked why she laughed, but she denied having done so. She was, after all, past child-bearing age. The man quietly repeated that she had laughed, and said: 'Is anything impossible with the Lord?'

The three now arose and made their way towards Sodom, where Lot made his home, near the gates of the city. They had heard terrible things about the evil magic practices of the city, and were going to see for themselves whether it was true. It had been said that, among other abominations, by coupling with animals, they had created creatures to serve them that were half man, half beast. Clearly, the world of gods and angels could not permit such things to continue.

Abraham knew that the fate of the Cities of the Plain now hung in the balance, and began to question his God: would He spare the city if there were fifty upright men living there, or even forty? Would the Lord spare the city for ten good men's sake? What about five? The Lord replied that He would spare the city if there were as many as five upright men living there.

When the three arrived at the gates of Sodom, Lot welcomed them in, advising them against entering the city. Almost at once, a gang of evil men, sensing the spiritual quality of the three, and wishing to use them for their dark magic, demanded that they come out. Lot tried to send them away, even offering them his daughters, instead, but the crowd was not to be appeased. Two of the three pulled Lot inside and caused the men of the crowd to become confused, so that they could no longer find the door.

The three now told Lot that he should gather his family together and all his goods and belongings, and leave the city, as it was to be destroyed. They should all go, and not look backward when they went.

The destruction of the cities of the plain

Lot gathered his family and servants and worldly goods together, and they set out, away from the city. Lot's wife, however, turned to look back the way they had come, and at once she became smitten with arthritic pains among her bones; the arteries and veins of her body became stiff and sclerotic, and it was said that she had become like a pillar of salt.

But God's judgment was upon the cities of the plain, and fire and brimstone rained down upon Sodom and Gomorrah. The lush, verdant plain of Jordan became a rocky wilderness, and the Cities of the Plain were destroyed.

Abraham went up to a high place and saw the destruction. Sadly he turned away, and moved his great camp onwards into the Negeb, where Abimelech ruled. Like Pharaoh before him, Abimelech saw Sarah, and took her into his household, believing her to be Abraham's sister. Abraham, wishing to avoid all strife, allowed this to happen, trusting in the Lord his God to make all right. This time, the Lord came to Abimelech in a dream and told him who Sarah was. Abimelech at once sent Sarah back to Abraham, with gifts of livestock and slaves. Abraham prayed to Jahweh on behalf of Abimelech that he and his household should not suffer, for the women of Abimelech's family had become barren once Sarah had been brought in among them. Jahweh answered Abraham's prayer, and the fertility of Abimelech's women was restored. More than this; Sarah at last conceived and gave birth to a son, Isaac.

Now, the sign of Abraham's covenant with his God was that all the males of his household should be circumcised. After eight days, Isaac was circumcised, and Sarah saw Hagar, once again, laughing in scorn. Sarah demanded that Hagar be sent away, and thus it was that Hagar and Ishmael left the camp of Abraham early one morning, with a few provisions and a skin full of water.

When the skin was empty, Hagar set Ishmael down under a bush, and walked away from him, weeping at their plight, for the length of two bowshots. As before, Hagar was approached by an angel who told her to go back and pick up her infant son, who was crying under the bush. The angel also showed her a well nearby, where she was able to refill the water skin. The child enjoyed the favour of God and became a mighty archer, and the father of a great race. Many Moslems today trace their origins and those of their Prophet from Ishmael.

The sacrifice and the founding of Jerusalem

Now the time came that Abraham understood that his son was to be a sacrifice to his God. He knew no other form than the blood sacrifice, and set off with wood for a fire and Isaac at his side.

Eventually they came to a hill where Abraham began to make ready, though with a heavy heart.

'Father, here is the wood, but where is the beast that we must sacrifice?' asked Isaac. Abraham replied: 'God will provide the sacrifice.' Then, he bound Isaac, and placed him on the stone altar. He drew his knife, and when Isaac felt the metal on his neck, he fell into a deathly swoon.

Then, from the realm of the Cherubim, Abraham heard a voice telling him to stay his hand, and not to touch the boy. There, in a thicket, a ram was caught fast by the horns, and this was the beast that should be offered up on the altar. But Abraham was blessed by God for his willingness to sacrifice what he held most dear in the world, though this was a sacrifice that was not desired of God.

On the same day that Isaac was offered to God, so an old legend tells, twelve Priest Kings came to Melchizedek and asked him to come to go with them. Melchizedek explained that he could not go to another place. Here was where he belonged. The twelve then held a solemn council together and decided that a city should be built there, for Melchizedek was the greatest among them, and of the kings of the earth. And so it came about that a city was raised up in that place by order of the twelve. Abraham had called the place Jare or 'God appears' but Melchizedek insisted that the place should bear the name of peace, or 'Salem'. So the city was called 'God appears in peace', or Jerusalem. Thus, an old legend tells of twelve builder Priest-Kings gathering around their master to build a city on sacred ground.

Sarah was very old when she passed away; she lived to the age of a hundred and twenty seven. Abraham made sure that the very best grave was found for her. He bought the plot from a Hittite prince. Melchizedek was present at the funeral. Kings and princes came to mourn Sarah as she was buried in a cave in Machpelah, east of the grove of terebinths, in Hebron.

Abraham married again and had more children, but did not live long thereafter. It was said that he was the first man ever to show the signs of age: grey hair and lined skin. Before he died, he made sure that a wife was found for Isaac. She was Rebecca, a beautiful maiden of Aram-Naharaim, and thus the line of descent continued from Abraham, the Father of a Host of Nations.

†

The carving in the chapel, opposite the carving of Melchizedek, is much damaged, and now, all that remains to be clearly seen is the ram of the sacrifice. In the north aisle, almost opposite, is the Agnus Dei, the Lamb of God; sign of a still greater sacrifice.

The sacrifical ram caught in the bush. Abraham and Isaac have been removed.

Melchizedek

The Horned Moses with Tablets of the Law and Staff of Jethro.

6. Moses

Many pulpits in churches, for instance, in North Germany, are supported by a statue of a horned Moses. Michelangelo's statue in Rome is probably the best known representation of this, where the horns seem like organs of sense, feeling their way into the world. In Rosslyn, the carving in the window shows Moses, holding the tablets of the law in his right hand, and the priestly staff that he received from Jethro in his left. His horns, though, are set back on his temples, and rise more like those of a cow than a ram, which would be the usual representation. In Rosslyn, the carving reminds us that Moses was, first, a priest of Isis, a son of the widow; Isis being often represented with the horns of a cow encircling a sun disc. The tablets of the law show the new direction to be taken by the Habiru, or Hebrew people, and the staff that the new direction is indeed continuous with the flow of destiny that began with Adam's expulsion from Eden. Opposite the carving of Moses, a helmeted angel offers the heart of Robert the Bruce, in homage to the leader who brought a new impulse into the moral life of the world and who brought a new emphasis to the life of thought.

The birth and childhood of Moses

There lived in Egypt, in the time of the Pharaohs, a brotherhood of free people, made up of many nationalities, close to the city of Thebes. These were the Pious of the Land, honourable people who turned their back on the decadent and cruel excesses of Egypt's rulers of the time.

Among these was a man named Amram, and a woman of the Habiru, or Hebrew people, named Jochebed, who had a child after seven months' pregnancy. At that time, most of the Habiru people lived in the Valley of Goshen, east of the Nile delta, where they lived as slaves, subject to the cruelties of their masters. The Habiru people had lived in Egypt for some four hundred years, since the time of Joseph, and were sometimes called the sons of Jacob, or the sons of Israel. But Jochebed lived among the pious brethren, far south of the delta.

At the birth, the chamber where she lay was filled with light, as though sun and moon shone together. Though premature, the child, a boy, was a sturdy and robust infant, and the leaders of the Pious of the Land knew that here was an important individual, who should be brought up within the precincts of the Temple.

Miriam, a young woman of the pious brethren, was sent to meet Bathia, the daughter of Pharaoh, who would adopt the child into the royal household. Miriam waited for Bathia by the waters of the Nile. The day was hot, and to shield the boy from the heat of the sun, he was placed in a tightly woven cradle of rushes, floating on the river water, which reflected the sunlight in ever-moving fiery glints. Bathia arrived, stooped and picked up the infant boy, saying: 'Look, I have rescued thee out of the water.'

It was agreed that Bathia would adopt the boy, and that his mother Jochebed would be his nurse, and Miriam, who was taken to be his sister, attend upon him. Thus it was that the boy grew up as a member of the royal household, and was trained in the priesthood of Osiris. His name was Hosarsiph. He was taken to the city of Heliopolis, known in the Bible as On, to be taught by wise men from all over the Mediterranean basin: Hellenes, Chaldeans and Egyptian priests of Osiris. There he learned the secret of the threefold writing: to write simply and literally; to write figuratively and symbolically; to write in a way that veiled the higher truth. Thus, the priests of Egypt could write a text that was literal, metaphorical and transcendent all at once. This he was able to use later, when he had undergone more powerful experiences.

It was part of the arrogance of the Pharaohs, and a symbol of their decadence, that they took themselves to be Initiates of the Mysteries of Osiris, to the extent that they claimed to be the replacement at the side of the goddess Isis for the slain Osiris. Hosarsiph, however, now a grown man, had looked deep into the mysteries, and knew that Isis remained a widow, silent and wordless, and that the soul of humanity still longed in its deepest being for the return of the goddess's consort. Those who had this experience consciously of the silent and grieving Isis were known as 'Sons of the Widow', a term that was to remain through long ages among the initiated.

The flight of Moses

One day, when Hosarsiph was in his fortieth year, he chanced to be passing some building works. There he saw what was after all, in those days, a common enough sight: an overseer mercilessly thrashing a Habiru slave. All at once, he became aware as never before of a division within himself. The Egyptian in him was offended by the thrashing, but accepted it as part of the world to which he belonged. The Habiru in him was filled with rage, not only at the overseer, but at the part of himself that closed its eyes to the fact; that accepted without question a privileged existence in a world maintained at the expense of those who are unfree. It became necessary in that instant, to kill the Egyptian within himself, but the outer expression of this inner resolve was that he slew the overseer.

Hosarsiph fled Egypt, making for the land of Midian. He took refuge with a wise old African priest, by the name of Jethro. In the threefold account that he made of his sojourn with Jethro the Ishmaelite, he tells how, while resting by a well, the seven daughters of this priest came to draw water to fill the troughs for their father's sheep, but shepherds came to chase them from the well. Hosarsiph took the girls' side, and drew water for the sheep himself. Thus, their father asked them to invite him to eat with them.

During his time with Jethro, Hosarsiph knew that he had to do penance for the Egyptian overseer whom he had slain. Jethro took him to a cave where Hosarsiph was to fall into a deep sleep in which he left his body to seek the souls of those who had died, but were still tied to the earthly realm. There he had to seek out the soul of the slain overseer, ask his forgiveness, and show him the way out of the bonds of the earthly sphere, and direct him towards the light of the higher spiritual worlds.

As highly initiated as he was, this was still no easy task for Hosarsiph, but after some time, it was done, and he emerged from the cave quite changed. To mark this change in himself, he now called himself 'Moses', the rescued one.

Moses married Zipporah, one of Jethro's daughters, and had a son by her called Gershom. Meanwhile, he worked as a shepherd for his father-in-law. One day, he saw a bush, all in flames, but the fire did not consume the bush. He went closer, but was stopped by a voice that told him to approach no nearer, and to take off his sandals, for he was in a holy place. This angelic voice identified itself as the God of Abraham, Isaac and Jacob. Filled with fear, Moses knelt, covering his face. The angel instructed Moses to return to Egypt to lead the children of Israel, the Habiru, out of bondage.

'Who am I, that I should go to Pharoah and lead the Israelites out of captivity?' asked Moses. The angel replied: 'I am with you. Bring the children of Israel to this place, to worship God on this mountain.'

'But if I go to the Habiru and say that the God of their forefathers has sent me to lead them, and they ask me His name, what shall I reply?'

'I am that I am,' the angel answered: 'Tell them that I AM has sent you to them, and His name is Jahweh. Jahweh is the God of Abraham, Isaac and Jacob, and say also that the God of their fathers has seen their suffering and heard their lamentation, and shall lead them out of Egypt into a land of milk and honey.'

Moses recognized this God, the I AM. Osiris was, for the Egyptians, the countenance of this God, and Moses knew the Egyptian mysteries well. This God was coming closer to the world and to human beings, though the journey would be long.

The return to Egypt

It is said that Moses was forty years with Jethro. Now he left to fulfil the task laid upon him by the God who spoke to him from the burning bush, even though he had no faith in the power of his words to move Pharaoh. Sure enough, at first Pharaoh made the tasks of the children of Israel yet heavier than they had been before, but now Moses had the help of a brother initiate from the ranks of the Habiru, Aaron.

He also had with him a staff given to him by Jethro, to help him accomplish his mighty tasks (see Chapter 2). This staff, it was said, had belonged to Seth, the son of Adam. Seth passed it on to Enoch, who gave it to Noah, who gave it to his son Shem, and his descendants, until it came into the hands of Abraham. From Abraham it went to Isaac, who passed it on to his son Jacob, who valued it above all other objects. When Jacob journeyed to Egypt to visit his son Joseph, he gave Joseph the staff as something of greater value than anything that he had given Joseph's brothers. On Joseph's death, the staff was passed on to the priests of Midian. Jethro was the greatest of these. When he received the staff, we are told that he planted it in his garden.

In the threefold language in which he later recorded the story of the exodus from Egypt, Moses described how he and Aaron tried to persuade Pharaoh to let the children of Israel leave their life of slavery. First came a fierce debate with the priests of Egypt, which is given in the picture of the priests each throwing down his staff, which then turned into a serpent. Moses met this by throwing down his own staff, which, also became a serpent, and devoured the other serpents. However, this did not persuade Pharaoh.

There then follows the tale of the Ten Plagues. In the face of Pharaoh's obduracy, Moses turned the waters of the Nile and the drinking water into blood. Still Pharaoh refused to let the Habiru go. There followed a plague of frogs, then of maggots, of flies, a pestilence that attacked and killed livestock, a thick layer of dust, outbreaks of fierce boils on the Egyptians' skin, hailstorms that destroyed growing crops, and an east wind bringing a cloud of locusts that devoured those crops not affected by the hail. None of these pestilences affected the children of Israel in the Valley of Goshen.

Still Pharaoh refused to allow the children of Israel to leave. Moses then gave clear instructions to the Habiru to take a sacrificial lamb and smear its blood on the doorposts and lintels, to roast and eat the lamb, burning any remains, and leave nothing of it behind. The lamb was to be eaten with unleavened bread and bitter herbs; all this in preparation for a terrible scourge that would affect the first-born of the Egyptians.

That night, the Angel of Death moved through Egypt, passing by the households where the doorposts and lintels were marked with the blood of the sacrificial lamb, but striking the first-born of Egypt.

The exodus from Egypt

At last Pharaoh's obstinacy gave way. His army at the time was fighting away to the west of Egypt, and he did not have the resources to stop the great caravan of people and livestock that started eastwards, towards the land of the promise. Moses, Aaron and Miriam led the great procession towards the land that they hoped to make their home.

They continued eastwards until they arrived at a finger of the Red Sea, known as the Sea of Reeds, somewhat to the west of the Gulf of Aqaba. Here they made camp, but became aware that they were being pursued by Pharaoh's army, now returned from battle, and sent after them as Pharaoh's need for vengeance for loss of face grew savage within him.

Moses saw that, with the movements of the tides and the way the east wind was blowing, an opportunity had arisen for them to pass through the Sea of Reeds safely. At first the people were afraid to take the risk, but one young man among them waded out, and the others gradually followed his example, and the children of Israel crossed the Sea of Reeds without mishap.

By the time Pharaoh's army arrived at the shore, the wind had dropped and the tide was on the turn. So, when they attempted the same route through the waters, they perished.

The people that Moses, Aaron and Miriam led did not yet know what to make of their leader, and whether to trust him. Thus the way was beset with quarrels and arguments, but always Moses managed to show strong leadership, and brought them to Sinai, where Jethro, Zipporah and the two sons of Moses, Gershom and Eliezer, met them. Moses greeted his father-in-law with extreme respect and reverence, and showed in his record of those times how it was the advice of Jethro that made him a more efficient and effective leader by teaching him how to delegate and mandate tasks among those able to take on such work

The great caravan of the Habiru people had been joined by others on the way that had not undergone the slavery in Egypt, or the hazards of the journey. These had a powerful influence on the children of Israel, and while Moses was on the mountain in solemn communion with his God, Aaron found himself at a loss to know how to direct the yearning of the people for a god that they could understand, and bowed to pressure to make something that the people could at least see. After they had crossed the Sea of Reeds, they had been led by a pillar of cloud by day and a column of fire by night, but the notion of a god for whom there are no pictures or effigies possible was too abstract for them to grasp. So Aaron gathered gold and jewellery from the people and caused to be made a calf of gold, which the people then worshipped, led by the example of Moabite women who had joined them, and were known for their sinuous beauty and their ability to dance in a way that fired the admiration and appetites of the men.

The golden calf and the Ark of the Covenant

When Moses came down from the mountain, he was horrified and outraged at what he saw, and acted quickly to destroy the golden calf and to rout, with a sternness that could appear cruel, those who had instigated this turning away from the God who had led them from captivity towards the task that was to take them many generations to fulfil. During his sojourn on the mountain, Moses had received the inspirations that made clear what the law should be, and what were the tenets and instructions by which the society, whose leader he was, should conduct their lives. Chief among these was the Decalogue, the Ten Commandments at the basis of the Law. Moses had carved these on two tablets of stone, which, when he saw the dancing in worship of the golden calf, he dashed to pieces on the rocks.

Once the unruly elements had been purged from the great camp, Moses again went up the mountain, and remained there for forty days and nights, fasting as he communed with his God. When he returned, bearing the newly made tablets of the law, he appeared to his people as though illuminated from within.

While in communion with God on Mount Sinai, Moses received strict and detailed instructions for the construction of an ark, made of acacia wood, and plated with gold, decorated with precious stones, and covered with fine cloth. It was to be further embellished with two gold cherubim at each end of the ark, with wings outspread and pointing upwards. Their wings would act as a screen over the cover. The Lord commanded Moses: 'Put the cover above the Ark, and put into the Ark the tokens that I shall give you. It is there that I shall meet you, and from above the cover, between the two cherubim over the Ark of the Tokens, I shall deliver to you all my commandments for the Israelites.'

This mysterious structure, designed to be carried by four men as the Israelites journeyed through the wilderness, was to be the outward sign of the promise God made to the Children of Israel, and came to be known as the Ark of the Covenant. It was to accompany them wherever they went. There were ceremonies to be observed whenever the Ark was approached, and these were to be rigidly followed, otherwise, the consequences were drastic. The Ark of the Covenant became the central focus for the Israelites through all their wandering, and remained so when their great pilgrimage came to an end in the Land of Canaan. Through it, God spoke to them.

Moses never saw his people arrive in the Land of the Promise. He died after forty years wandering in the desert. Moses was forty years in Egypt, forty years with Jethro and the priests of Midian, and forty years in the desert. No doubt the fires of life energy burned in him with a bright Zarathustra-like flame, but perhaps this time of forty years denotes something beyond simply the passage of a given time.

The death of Moses

When the Children of Israel finally became settled in the Promised Land, King David wished to build a temple to house the Ark of the Covenant, but this he was never to achieve. It was Solomon who was to carry this out, and then only with the help of a neighbouring king. The next chapter tells that story. The Temple of Solomon took forty years to build, and was representative of the transformation in the souls of those who strove to build it. Perhaps behind these stages of forty years is concealed the time in which an important inner transformation is accomplished? No doubt the children of Israel went through an important change during the time of their wandering, as they grew from an enslaved people to the bearers of a vital new impulse and possibility in the world; the development of abstract thought.

What became of the Ark after the second destruction of the Temple in Roman times? No-one can say for sure, but a strange rumour describes how it was discovered, and taken, with an escort of Templar Knights, deep into the mountains of Ethiopia, where, according to some explorers, it remains to this day, still a potent and mysterious thing.

7. The Temple of Solomon

Rosslyn is built on the site of an old Temple of Mithras, a remnant of the Roman occupation (see also Chapter 8). Mithras worship began in Persia, and was a rigorously demanding process of initiation that bound Roman soldiers together in a military brotherhood in something of the same way that soldiers in Victorian times had Masonic Lodges specifically for military men, regardless of rank. Temples of Mithras were generally subterranean constructions, and thus it is that Rosslyn goes down into the ground as high as it rises above it. The existence of vaulted passages under the chapel is well known; the Sinclairs were laid there in their armour from its beginning until the year 1650.

There are, as we have noticed elsewhere in this work, all the signs of Templar influence in the building of the chapel, and the existence of the underground spaces that once were dedicated to Mithras took on a different identity when they became the vaults of Rosslyn. Those Templars who excavated beneath the Temple of Solomon in Jerusalem took away with them certain things that they found there — no-one really knows what — and there is a tradition that these things were hidden in the vaults of Rosslyn: further, that this was the chief function and purpose of the chapel, to be a worthy place of concealment for those finds. No searches beneath the chapel so far have been able to discover any such treasure, but such investigations as have been conducted certainly show the presence of something below the floor.

Christopher Knight and Robert Lomas argue in several of their published works that Rosslyn is intended to be homage, conscious and deliberate, to the Temple of Solomon, as it was found by the Templars in 1118, and that the west wall of Rosslyn is a sort of Gothic version of the Wailing Wall in Jerusalem. Rosslyn is by no means a copy of the original Temple; rather it is an imaginative reconstruction, using techniques and forms available to the builders in the fifteenth century.

Certainly, the builders, the craftsmen and masons who raised the chapel had a mythology at the centre of the mystery of their craft, and this was based on the awareness of a long connection with the building of the first Temple of Solomon. The Master Craftsmen all knew the story of the building of the Temple, and it was passed on to the journeymen and apprentices when they were deemed worthy to receive it. It was at the heart of their work, all through the forty years that the chapel was in construction. This is the story that they knew.

Fourteen generations after Abraham came King David. David's wish at the end of his days was to build a temple to hold the Ark of the Covenant, but he was unable to encompass this in his lifetime. The legends suggest that David wished to make his peace with his God through the building of a place of worship. But he was unable to build the temple as his attention was forcibly diverted by various wars and strife. The building of the

The Zerubabel architrave.

temple was a task taken up by Solomon, the son of David and Bath-Sheba. In order to do this, he was forced to call upon the skills and experience of a man from a neighbouring country, Hiram Abiff.

But the story of the building of the Temple of Solomon starts with the very beginnings of the world, as told in the legends of the Freemasons.

The building of the Temple of Solomon

In the early days of the world, the Angelic beings of the order known as the Elohim created Eve, and they fathered Cain on her. Adonai-Jahweh created Adam. Adam and Eve became man and wife, and Eve gave birth to their son Abel.

Cain worked the land, while Abel was a shepherd. Cain transformed what he found, while Abel took the world as he found it. Cain's sacrifice was rejected by Adonai-Jahweh, though Abel's was accepted. In jealous rage, Cain slew Abel, and thus Mother Earth lost her innocence as the first drops of blood shed in anger fell on to her soil. After this, Adam and Eve had another son, Seth.

After many great ages had passed, Solomon the son of David became the King of the Children of Israel. He wished to complete the work that his father David wished to see accomplished: the building of the Temple of the Lord. But Solomon, of the bloodline of Seth, brother of Abel, had no-one in his kingdom with the wisdom or knowledge necessary for such a task. He sent to the King of Tyre, Hiram, for help. Hiram of Tyre sent one of his subjects to undertake the work for Solomon. This man was Hiram Abiff, of the race of Cain, and the son of a widow. And so the work began.

Now, Balchis, the Queen of the South, from the land of Sheba, came to Solomon. She was led into his presence, and beheld him seated on his throne, where she took him for a wonderful statue of gold and ivory. Solomon's glory impressed her deeply, and soon, they exchanged rings as a token of promise to each other.

Balchis wished to see the temple that was being constructed, and Solomon led her there. She expressed the desire to see all the men employed in building the temple. Solomon said that this was not possible, but Hiram Abiff climbed on to a small promontory and made the sign of the Tau. The workers, seeing this sign, stopped their labours and gathered round him.

If Balchis had been impressed by Solomon, it was a different feeling that awoke in her on seeing Hiram. Her heart kindled towards him, and Solomon noticed this, and jealousy began to poison his heart.

The three journeymen

The work on the Temple progressed, including the two pillars Jachin and Boaz, to the left and right of the entrance to the Temple. But there were fifteen workers, journeymen who wished to be given the Master Word, and thus promoted to the full mystery of their crafts. These fifteen came to Hiram, who begged them to be patient; that they would, in course, be promoted in their just degree. Twelve of the journeymen were satisfied with this, but three were angry and whispered together against Hiram, vowing revenge.

Their plotting was overheard by a young apprentice called Benoni, who went to Solomon straight away to warn him. Solomon, already listening to the promptings of jealousy, did nothing.

The three, Fanor the Syrian mason, Amru the Phoenician carpenter and Methusael the Hebrew miner, knew that a great work was in hand, the casting of the Molten Sea. This was a mighty work to stand in the Temple precincts, and would show, in a dynamic form of different metals, movement in stillness. It was in the form of a lily, and rested on the backs of twelve sculpted bulls. The casting of this demanded the most careful handling; the mixing of the metals had to be done with the strictest precision. The three interfered with the work so that the molten metals spread over the rim of the cast, endangering those who watched. Hiram tried desperately to stem the molten tide using water, but this only made matters worse. A deadly rain of boiling water and molten metal fell in hissing clouds, and the people fled before the catastrophe.

Hiram, in the midst of his despair, suddenly heard a voice: it was his ancestor, Tubal Cain, calling him and telling him to dive into the flames.

'Come, my son. Be without fear. I have rendered thee impervious to fire. Cast thyself into the flames.'

'Where do you take me?'

'Into the centre of the Earth, the soul of the world, into the Kingdom of great Cain, where liberty reigns with him. There the tyranny of Adonai ceases. There we can be, despising his anger. We can taste the fruit of the Tree of Knowledge. There is the home of thy fathers.'

'Who, then, am I? And who are you?'

'I am the father of thy fathers. I am the son of Lamech. I am Tubal Cain.'

Hiram was led to the presence of Cain, the author of his race, who appeared surrounded by a light like that of Lucifer, Son of the Morning. He was told by the son of Tubal Cain and Naamah that he, Hiram Abiff, would have a son, whom he would not see, but whose descendants would perpetuate his race.

Hiram was at last restored to the more familiar surroundings of the Temple precincts. He had been given the hammer and the help of the genii of fire, to put right the molten sea. This he accomplished in a single night, and the people were happy to see it. Balchis exulted.

Hiram Abiff and Balchis

One day after this, Balchis and her nurse Sarahil were walking, and they came in sight of Hiram. In the course of his work, he made again the sign of the Tau, and Had-Had, the hoopoe, a particular pet of Balchis, flew up, circled Hiram's head three times, and alighted on his wrist. When Sarahil saw this, she exclaimed: 'The oracle is fulfilled! Had-Had recognizes the husband which the genii of fire destined for Balchis. She dare accept the love of none but him!'

This was in harmony with the promptings of her heart, but Balchis had exchanged rings with Solomon. She was able, while the King was overcome with wine, to take the ring from his finger, and so she was free to accept the love of Hiram.

When Solomon awoke, he noticed the loss and guessed what had happened. In his jealousy, he hinted that if there were any who wished Hiram harm, he would do nothing to prevent it. This the three journeymen learned, and they lay in wait for Hiram. They took up their places each by a gate of the Temple precincts, the gates called Strength, Beauty and Wisdom. It was Hiram's custom to worship the Most High, and knowing this, they lay in wait.

Hiram came to leave by the east gate, where the first of the journeymen accosted him, demanding to be given the Master Word and the secret of the Shamir, the stone-splitting serpent. Again, Hiram told him that his patience and industry would be rewarded when the time was ripe. The journeyman struck Hiram a blow to the throat with a twenty-four inch gauge. Hiram fell to his left knee, but raised himself up and fled to the south gate. There the next journeyman awaited him, and angrily demanded the same as the first. Hiram again refused, and was struck a second time, and he fell to his right knee. He ran to the west gate, passing by the well, dropping in to it as he passed the golden triangle that he wore round his neck, with the Master Word engraved on it. At the last gate, however, he was accosted for the third time and struck again with a gavel to the right temple. Now he fell dead. Thus, Balchis, the Queen of Sheba, was widowed, and the son of Hiram was in truth a Son of the Widow.

The three now hastened to rid themselves of the body of Hiram, carrying it out by the west gate, and dug a shallow grave in the side of a hill. One placed a branch of acacia over the place where they buried Hiram; then they fled.

The discovery of the body of Hiram

After seven days, Solomon was forced to agree to send a party to search for Hiram, whose life was by now despaired of. Foul play was suspected, and it was agreed to change the Master Word to the first word that was spoken when the body of Hiram was discovered. Twelve of the most trusted of the crafts were sent out, three to the north, three to the south, three to the east and three to the west.

They found his corpse beneath the acacia, and attempted to lift it with the grip known to the members of Hiram's craft. But as they moved the body, the flesh fell away. One said: 'Macbenach!' ('The flesh is off the bones!' Or, according to others, 'The brother is smitten!') This now became the new Master Word. Only the Master grip, the Lion Grip, could be used to lift the body.

In time, the heads of the three were brought to Solomon. The golden triangle, too, was discovered, and Solomon caused it to be placed on a triangular altar set up in a secret vault beneath the most retired part of the temple. This triangular altar was further concealed by a cubical stone on which was engraved the sacred law of Moses.

None but the twenty-seven elect of the crafts knew where the altar stood. When all was done, the place was walled up.

Zerubabel and the rebuilding of the Temple

The temple, then, was built in the midst of severe tensions and tragedy. Fourteen generations after the temple was built, it was destroyed by the Babylonians, who came to carry the children of Israel into captivity, into the land of Babylon, or Persia.

Now, many years later, in the days of King Darius, the Hebrews had become assimilated in various ways into the life of Persia, but had not abandoned their God or their way of life. One man had risen to an important position in the court of Darius, and this was Zerubabel, who was an important and trusted member of the king's bodyguard.

One day, King Darius summoned his bodyguards, and set them the task of deciding the following question: What is the strongest power in the world? The answers were to be written, and put under his pillow, as he slept. Thus Darius was able to test, not only the wisdom of the men whom he most needed to trust — so close were they to his royal personage, and armed at all times — but also their literacy, and their ability to enter his chamber silently, without waking him.

The bodyguards went their separate ways to consider the question, and to make ready for the task of silently entering the king's sleeping quarters. As the night wore on, three of them succeeded in placing their answer under the king's pillow.

In the morning, the king summoned his household, and demanded of each man to justify his choice of the strongest power. The first man had written: Wine, for it could scatter the wits of all; even, he dared to suggest, the king himself. It could lay strong men low, and rob them of their memory.

Darius then called upon the next to substantiate his claim, which was for the king himself.

The second man stood and told the audience that no man had more power than the king: he could ordain the life or death of any in his realm; he was chosen and blessed by the gods, and none could gainsay him.

Darius now summoned Zerubabel to defend his answer, which was twofold.

'There is a power yet greater than the king,' said Zerubabel. 'I have seen the king subordinate his power to a pretty woman, doing all he could to satisfy her smallest whim. Therefore, I say that women are a strong power in the world, but I say this as well: that truth bears all away before it; the strength of kings, the wishes of women, and even the effects of wine are as nothing before the power of truth.'

'I like this answer well,' said Darius, 'and I give you the prize. Ask me what you will, and I shall reward you with your heart's desire.'

'Truly, you are a wise and just king,' said Darius, 'and if you grant me my heart's desire, you are indeed great among the kings of the world. For know, O king, that my greatest wish is to return to the city of Jerusalem with others of my people, there to rebuild the Temple that was built by Solomon.'

The court was silent, waiting for Darius to speak. Would he be true to his word, or had the Hebrew demanded too much of a generous king?

Finally, Darius spoke. 'What I have promised I shall do,' he said. 'Zerubabel and his people shall indeed go to Jerusalem to rebuild the temple.'

So it was that a great procession of the Children of Israel returned to Jerusalem, singing and making music as they went, and when they arrived they set to work rebuilding the temple.

†

Some say that the carving in the south west of the chapel, high to the left over the door, is not the apprentice Tam Nimmo, but Hiram Abiff himself, with the first wound in his temple clearly marked. Looking at this carving, one can see where there is damage to the jaw. An apprentice would not have been permitted to grow a beard, and the carving could have had a beard smashed away. Another carving not far away is traditionally called 'The Widow', and associated with Tam Nimmo's mother. Could we also see Balchis in the sorrowing face?

Sadly, the rebuilt temple was not to last. In 70 AD, the Romans all but destroyed it. It was this ruin that the first Templar Knights discovered in the year 1118, but that belongs to another chapter.

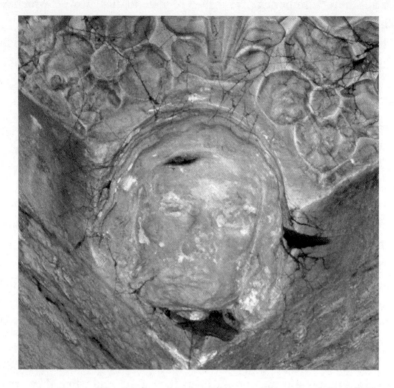

The Head of the Apprentice, said by some to be the head of Hiram Abiff. The wound to the upper right temple is clearly visible, and in Victorian times was picked out in red ochre paint.

8. Elijah

To the left of the Victorian baptistery, high on the external west wall there is a mutilated and weathered carving that represents Elijah's assumption into heaven in a fiery chariot. Although we are concentrating here mostly on the carvings inside the chapel, Elijah is too important a personality to miss out.

On the site of Rosslyn some two thousand years ago, there was a Roman temple of Mithras. The Biblical scholar and researcher Emil Bock pointed out a strong resonance between the Mithraic initiation and the life of Elijah. The initiation path followed by those Roman soldiers faithful to Mithras was sevenfold. First was the rank of Raven, or Corax; he who was open to the promptings of the spirit. Elijah's nourishment was brought from the skies by ravens. Second came the level of the Hidden One, or Occultus. We saw earlier how Elijah appeared sometimes through the voice of another, himself remaining hidden from the eyes of the people. The third rank was that of Soldier, or Miles. Elijah was indeed a warrior of the spirit. The fourth rank of initiation was that of the Lion, or Leo. This, in the story of Elijah, was represented by his entry into the cave, wherein he underwent a profound change. At the fifth stage of initiation, the postulant would be seen as a true representative of his people. As the Mithras initiation took its origin from Persia, the rank was called Persa, though for Elijah it would be a true Israelite, once he was sent to anoint the kings. For those soldiers camped in Scotland, their nationalities would have been honoured if any attained the fifth rank. There may even have been some true Scots among them. The sixth rank was that of Runner of the Sun, or Heliodromos. This is how Elisha experienced Elijah when he asked for the mantle of prophecy to pass to him. When Elijah did indeed let fall his mantle on to the shoulders of Elisha, he had attained the rank of Father, or Pater. 'My father, my father!' cried Elisha. 'The chariots of Israel and its horsemen!'

The story of Elijah

In the days when Ahab was king, he moved the centre of government from Jerusalem to Shechem. His queen, Jezebel, was a high priestess of the goddess Asherah, and instituted the worship of Baal and Asherah among the people. Many turned away from the worship of Jahweh, including the king.

This was a time of drought. The springs ran dry and the land became arid and barren, even the green fields around Galilee were affected. In these hard conditions, when food and drink was scarce, the people were astonished to see the prophet Elijah fed by ravens, who brought him sustenance.

Elijah was a great fiery force for righteousness in the land. His capacity to travel great distances was a riddle to many. The king, Ahab, was taken aback when Elijah appeared before him and spoke to him in a public place, saying: 'I swear that, unless I tell you otherwise, there shall be neither rain nor dewfall, by the life of the Lord God of Israel, whose prophet I am.'

Elijah then left Shechem and went to dwell by the stream of Kerith, where the ravens fed him, and the water still flowed for him to drink. Yet, in time, that too, dried up, for there was no rain. The power to influence the elements lay not in Elijah's hands. He could see that the time was not come that the people should turn away from their spiritual destiny and embrace the gods of others. The fact that this had happened brought about an imbalance in the spiritual worlds that transferred itself to the world of nature.

The word of God came to Elijah to leave that place and go to Zarephath on the coast. It was a long journey, and he felt the suffering of the people as he went, and did not hold himself aloof from it, but took it upon himself.

In Zarephath he took lodgings with a poor widow, whose sufferings during the time of drought were great.

'Woman, will you bring me a little water and a small cake of bread to eat?' he asked her. She wrung her hands and replied: 'Alas, I have only a handful of flour and a little water. A few drops of oil remain in the bottom of the flask. Even now I am fetching a few sticks with which to light a fire, but what I shall cook on the fire I cannot yet see.'

Elijah sympathized with her, and he said: 'Make me the cake, as I bid you. I promise that the flour shall not run out as long as the famine lasts, nor will the oil.'

She did as she was bidden, and it was as Elijah said; neither the flour nor the oil ran out while the troubles of the people lasted.

But now another calamity befell the woman. Her son, who was sick unto death, died. She came to Elijah in her grief, saying: 'I took you into my house, and you have shown up my sins to the Lord. Look, he is dead.'

Elijah took the body of the youth to the roof, and called upon the Lord God to help him. Then, he breathed upon the boy, and called him back to life. The youth lived indeed.

Now Jezebel the queen had caused many of the priests of Jahweh to be put to death, but there was a man in the household of King Ahab called Obadiah, and he worshipped Jahweh in secret, and arranged for many priests to be hidden away in safety, with enough food and drink to sustain them. Ahab now called Obadiah to search the kingdom for whatever food and victuals were to be found. It was while Obadiah was working at this task that he met Elijah, coming from Zarephath.

'Go to Ahab,' commanded Elijah, 'and tell him that the drought is coming to an end.'

Obadiah was horrified, anxious that a message from Elijah would betray him as a secret worshipper of Jahweh. His fears were overcome, however, and indeed, the drought came to an end, and the rain began to fall. But now Elijah stood up before the people and said to them: 'The time has come to choose. You cannot serve Jahweh and Baal. Let us see whose god is the more powerful. Let the priests of Baal place a quartered ox on their altar, and see if the fire comes from heaven to burn it, and I shall set up an altar in the place where the altar of the Lord God was torn down, and I shall place upon it a quartered ox, and call upon fire from heaven.'

Elijah and the priests of Baal

This was a challenge that the priests of Baal at once accepted. Their altars stood in fine temples, and the priestesses came and danced around them in yellow robes, tied at the waist with purple sashes, as they called down the fire from heaven. The priests wore blue robes as they invoked their gods to send fire from above. Meanwhile, Elijah went to the place where the ruins of the altar of Jahweh stood, and put together twelve rough stones, one for each of the twelve tribes of Israel, contrasting greatly with the smooth edifices of Baal and Asherah. Sing and dance as they might, no matter what throes of ecstasy they fell into, the priests and priestesses of Baal and Asherah were not rewarded with fire to burn their sacrifice. King Ahab watched with increasing dismay as the efforts of the Priests of Baal accomplished nothing.

'Sing a little louder,' called Elijah; 'Perhaps he cannot hear you. He is a god, and far away.'

Still they danced and sang; they beat themselves with swords and spears until their blood ran freely, but no fire fell from heaven.

'Is your god asleep?' called Elijah; 'is he away visiting other gods?'

All the ritual and blood-letting was in vain. No fire fell. Then it was his turn. Elijah called the people to follow him to where he had set up the altar of twelve rough stones. He ordered the people to pile the altar with sticks and to pour water over it all. This they did, and again Elijah commanded that water be poured over the whole. This, too, was done as he ordained, but he told them a third time to pour water over the altar and the sacrifice, which they did, until the trench that stood before the altar was filled with the water that overflowed. Then Elijah called on the Lord his God to send down the fire from heaven, and his prayer was answered.

Elijah then sent Ahab home, and sent his servant out to look for the signs of a coming rainstorm. The servant went out seven times, in all directions, before he could at last report that he saw a cloud no bigger than a man's hand in the west. At last, the storm came. The sky grew black with clouds, and Ahab rode his chariot to the city of Jezreel to report to the queen what had happened, but such was the power of the divine within him that Elijah arrived there before him.

The people were amazed, but Jezebel the queen was stricken with cold rage. She resolved there and then that she would have her revenge on this prophet. Elijah could read her heart, and, as the time of his mission was not yet done, he left the city and went south to Sinai, to commune with his God.

The journey took forty days and nights, during which time Elijah was fed through the help of an angel, who woke him to show him where food was lying waiting for him. Once arrived at the mountain where Moses had received the Tablets of the Law, he climbed to a high place. Here he experienced the fury and rage of the elements, but the voice of God was not in the whirlwind or the hurricane; the earthquake or the storm clouds or the thunder and lightning that crashed and rolled around him. Instead, when the storm was stilled, he heard a still, small voice speaking to him in the calm of his soul. He covered his face and went into the cave to listen, for this was the true voice of his God. After this, Elijah was transformed and his mission took on a new and sombre power.

What was revealed to Elijah in the cave in that holy place remains a secret, but what was revealed to the writers of the Scriptures was that he should go to Damascus and anoint Hazael to be king of Aram and Jehu to be king of Israel. Then he was to appoint Elisha as his successor. Terrible wars were to follow the appointments of these men as kings, but those who had not worshipped Baal were spared.

Naboth's vineyard and the end of Elijah

Now there lived in Jezreel a man by the name of Naboth who had inherited a vineyard that Ahab coveted, as it lay close to his palace grounds, and the soil was good and the vine plentiful and healthy. However, Naboth had no wish to sell his vineyard. The queen Jezebel had discovered something about Naboth. As an initiate of Asherah, she knew that Elijah sometimes spoke through Naboth; that he was inspired by the mighty spirit of Elijah, and was at times his spokesman. In a spirit of revenge, she colluded with Ahab on a plan that would send Naboth to his death. A feast was arranged at which Naboth should be the guest of honour, but two men were suborned to accuse him of cursing God and the king.

So it all took place as Jezebel had arranged. The feast went forward, and suddenly, the two criminals arose and accused Naboth of cursing God and Ahab. The crowd in a rage dragged Naboth out and stoned him to death.

Ahab was walking in his newly acquired vineyard some time later when Elijah appeared to him.

'Are you there again, my enemy? Have you found me?' said Ahab, much afraid. He knew that the vision of Elijah before him betokened his imminent death.

'I am here. I have found you indeed. And know that where the blood of Naboth was spilled; where the dogs licked it up; there shall your blood be licked up by the dogs. Your household shall perish and your queen be devoured by the dogs on the ramparts of Jezreel.'

Ahab was smitten with shame, and donned sackcloth and ashes and did penance before the Lord. This meant that though he was spared the destruction that Elijah had foretold, he still had not long to live, and the punishment later fell upon his son Ahaziah when he, though king of Israel, worshipped Baal, turning against the religion of his forefathers and his people.

It was Elisha who told of the end of Elijah. He had asked him that the greater part of his spirit should come to him when the time came for him to take up Elijah's mantle of prophecy. Elijah answered that this was a hard thing to promise, but that if Elisha saw him before he died, it would come to pass that he would inherit the greater part of his spirit.

Elisha was beside the River Jordan when he saw Elijah in a chariot all of fire, drawn by horses all of flame. Elisha knelt before this vision, and as Elijah rode overhead, he dropped his mantle so that it fell upon the shoulders of Elisha.

In a loud voice, Elisha cried: 'My father! Oh, my father!'

†

The spirit of Elijah lived on in Elisha, but was seen again in a different form when John the Baptist came to make straight the path of the Saviour. It is no coincidence that Elijah is seen above the baptistery that was added to Rosslyn in the nineteenth century. Just as his spirit lived again in John the Baptist, so his image is just discernible over the place of baptism in the chapel.

9. The Three Kings

In the Lady Chapel of Rosslyn, at the eastern end of the chapel, there are four pendent bosses. These are stalactite-like pieces of stone, carved for the most part with floral or plant motifs, but one shows the Mother and Child, looking southwards, towards the feminine side of the chapel, while the Three Kings face the congregation, looking westward. On the eastern side of the boss are the Shepherds who kept watch over their flocks on the hills where the terebinth trees of Mamre once grew. On the underside of the boss is an eight-pointed star, known in Rosslyn as the Star of Bethlehem. An ominous aspect of the boss is that, at the left shoulder of the Mother is the figure of Death, robed like a monk, holding a scythe. It seems that Death, too, came to worship at the cradle of the Christ-child, knowing that here was the One who would overcome him.

Rosslyn is the Collegiate Chapel of Saint Matthew, and it is in Matthew's Gospel that we read of the Three Kings of the Orient, who saw the Star in the east and came to worship the child born King of the Jews. It is their story that we shall now tell according to an old version of the legend.

The vision of the star

In the land of Morn, at the top of a high tower, built for observing the stars and their movements, stood Melchior, priest of Zarathustra. High above him, in the eastern skies, was a constellation of stars that had aroused in him deep wonder and a dawning hope, but he wanted to be perfectly sure that he truly understood what he saw.

Long years before Melchior, the priesthood of Zarathustra had been kings in the land. It had been in the full flame of its activity five thousand years before Troy fell to the Hellenes. Some said their wisdom and teaching was older than that of Egypt. In the time of Melchior, they were advisors and counsellors to kings, and highly revered men. But now, a star had appeared that promised the fruition of a long-held hope; the birth of a child of royal blood, in whom the mysteries of Ahura Mazdao would be fulfilled for all the world.

He looked again through the long optic tube — not a telescope, but a device designed to concentrate the observer's vision on one part of the sky — and confirmed in his own mind what it was he was looking at.

Then, all at once, his soul was filled with a vision: a woman who looked southwards in deep serenity, held at her breast a child, who turned his eyes to the east, so that the rising sun was reflected in his eyes. He knew from his familiarity with the ancient mysteries of Egypt that the woman was Isis, and the child Horus, but now the spouse of the widowed Isis was reborn in this child; it was as if she was no longer a widow.

He summoned the scholar Viligratia, who now came hastening up the stairs, laden with scrolls.

'What can you tell me of this star?' asked Melchior, as soon as Viligratia had got his breath back.

'Alas, I can tell you nothing from my own wisdom, but my learning informs me that this is indeed the sign that you think it is. The old books all agree.'

'Do they agree where the child shall be born?' demanded Melchior. To this, Viligratia was ready with an answer. The scriptures all agreed that it should be in the Land of Judah.

'I must seek out this child,' said Melchior. 'He must be recognized and welcomed into the world as a king.'

'But what shall you take as an offering?' asked Viligratia. This question had been occupying Melchior's mind, too. Finally he decided upon gold in the form of a finely-wrought crown, and leaving Viligratia to take over his duties during his absence, he set out, wrapping his red cloak about his shoulders, to find the place where the child had been born.

The constellation had been seen in Saba by a younger man of the same priesthood, an African by the name of Caspar. He had at once recognized what the star portended, and a blissful joy flooded his whole being that he had been alive to see the birth of the child of kingly blood.

'Look! See,' he told his servants gathered around him. 'The star itself calls me forth to seek the child and offer him my homage and reverence.'

The night before he set out, he dreamed of the destiny of the child, and awoke in a more solemn mood. Putting aside the gift that he had first thought to take, he chose instead myrrh, the bitter herb that was symbol of the death and resurrection of Osiris; the death of the lower life and the resurrection of the higher life through mastery of the deep mysteries of the will. Though a priest of Zarathustra, as an African he knew the meaning and universality of the mysteries of Egypt. Then, wearing his finest green robe, he set out.

The oldest of the priests of Zarathustra to celebrate the birth of the child was Balthazar, also of Saba. He had been alerted to wonders about to befall by watching the flight of birds, of listening to the wind in the trees and the waters of the streams in the mountains. All of nature was telling him to be ready for a great change. He listened to the sounds of the world around him, and sniffed the air. When he, too, looked up and saw the movement of the stars, it confirmed what he had suspected through the evidence of his senses.

There was no question for him in his mind about what he should take as an offering; his journeys in India had prepared him for this moment. Frankincense would be his gift. Dressed all in blue, he, too, set out to find the child.

The three kings meet

They had not travelled very far before Caspar and Balthazar met on the road. They did not, at first, give the true reason for their journey, yet they travelled onwards together, as two priests of the same mysteries.

It was not until they saw in the distance, a little after sunset one day, a small group of people camped round a fire by a well of sweet water. As they drew closer, Balthazar noticed the way the leader of the group looked at the fire, and occasionally looked up at the star in the east. Almost at once, he knew him for one of their own.

A servant boy came to Melchior to tell him of the approach of strangers, and the red-cloaked magus stepped forward to meet them. Caspar and Balthazar made their camp with Melchior, and the three sat by the fire and began to talk together of their journey and why they had each set forth. Melchior at once gave his reasons for travelling so far from home.

'The holy scriptures all agree that a child shall be born of a royal household, in whom the mysteries shall be fulfilled for all to witness. But see that star in the sky to the eastward? That is surely the sign that the child's birth is due. And so I am travelling to find the child to do him homage.'

'I, too, follow that star,' said Balthazar, 'and when I contemplate it, before my mind's eye there arises a vision of a maidenly girl with a child at her breast.'

Caspar felt the joy rising in his soul again. When he spoke, the words almost burst out of him.

'Why, sirs, this is most marvellous! I, too, have been summoned from my home by this star. We must be stirring with the very break of dawn to seek this child. And are we agreed where we should look?'

Balthazar spoke, saying that they should be searching in the Land of the Children of Israel, for it was among the Sons of King David that the child would be born. Melchior agreed, saying: 'We must make our way to Judea, and enquire at the royal palace in Jerusalem, for there is surely our journey's end.'

The next morning, with the enthusiasm of Caspar as the spur to busy activity, the caravan set off towards Judea, to find the son of the royal house of David. The journey was long, and over difficult country, but most difficult of all was that the nearer they drew to Jerusalem, the more obscured by dark clouds the star constellation in the east became.

Herod's court

It was the day upon which King Herod heard the pleas of the people, setting himself up in the seat of Solomon to pass judgment on those who came before him. His servant came to him quite discomposed in manner, nervous and flustered, to announce that three noblemen had arrived from far countries, seeking special audience with the king. Though normally at ease in his own surroundings, Herod felt a spasm of fear crush his heart for a second.

'Who are they? What are they like? Bring me more information,' he ordered his servant, who ran to do Herod's bidding. During his absence, Herod felt the fear in his heart grow and recede, grow and recede with each heartbeat. At last the servant returned, apparently reassured.

'They are three priests of the Fire Mysteries of their God, Ahura Mazdao; two from Saba, one from Morn. They look for your help, Your Majesty, in a matter that they feel you alone can arrange for them.'

Herod's fear gave way to simple curiosity. Here, then, was no threat; simply another opportunity to demonstrate his power and munificence. He gave orders for them to be admitted, and sat in his judgment seat, composing himself.

The three entered, looking about them with interest. One, the eldest, the white-bearded man in blue, looked at Herod, and held back a little from the royal greetings, watching the King of Judea closely. It was Caspar who spoke for all three.

'We are searching for the child who is born the King of the Jews, for we have seen his star rising in the eastern skies.'

Herod's expression betrayed his ignorance of the events that Caspar described. Caspar leaned forward, entreating the king to listen carefully to what he had to say.

'And we have come to do Him homage and reverence in His own country,' he concluded. Herod bowed, and excused himself for a minute or two, as he drew his servant aside, out of the hearing of the three.

'What do we know of this? And why is it known to these foreigners? Why, above all, is it not known to me?'

The servant was unable to answer, as much from fear of the king as his own ignorance in the matter. Herod whispered in his servant's ear again.

'Fetch me some priests who can tell me something of this, as quick as you can! Go!'

The servant left, and Herod turned again to the three.

'Sirs,' he began, 'I confess I know as little of the newly born king as you do yourselves. What can you tell me of him, and his star?'

Caspar and Melchior told Herod as much as they could of the star, of what their scriptures, and others from other ancient traditions indicated of this child and His destiny. Balthazar kept as silent as he could, watching Herod with reserve. Herod asked particularly when the star appeared, and how long they could expect to see it in its present form, weighing their answers carefully. He kept the three at his palace for some days, asking them questions, and comparing their answers with what the priests that he had summoned had to say. The priests, he noticed, could only parrot what their scriptures said, and showed no penetration of their meaning, as opposed to these three foreign noblemen, who clearly understood what study and observation had revealed to them. What he did manage to glean from the priests, however, was that their parrotings of the prophets and the testimony of the three eastern noblemen agreed in the principal matter: a child was due to be born of the royal house of David, who would be a great king, and that the signs and portents indicated that His time was come.

At last Herod dismissed the three, saying: 'When you have found Him and offered Him your gifts, return and let us know where He is to be found, as we, too would welcome Him and do Him reverence.'

No sooner had the three left Herod's presence than the king began to rail and shout, roundly abusing his servants and household. Here was a threat to his crown, and it took a party of foreign priests to alert him to the fact. He paced the corridors of the royal palace, desperately trying to think of a way to deal with this menace. At last, he summoned the Captain of the Guard.

The finding of the child

Melchior spoke as the three made their way out of the city of Jerusalem: 'Herod is not of the House of David. We must seek the descendants of Jesse, David and Solomon, for it is among them that we shall find the child.'

A group of men went past, dressed all in white, unbleached clothes. These were members of the Essenes; devout people who generally maintained their existence apart from the world, in communities that ate no flesh and drank no strong drink. Balthazar approached these men and began to question them as the shadows lengthened through the city and night began to fall. After a short conversation, he rejoined Caspar and Melchior.

'We should make our way to Bethlehem, to the house of a pious and righteous man who is descended directly from Solomon, David and Jesse. His name is Joseph bar Jacob, and his wife has recently given birth to their son.'

Bethlehem lay a little way south of the city of Jerusalem, and the nearer they drew to the small township, the brighter the star shone, now no longer obscured by the dark clouds. Once arrived in the town, they took their beasts to the stable of an inn; a cave hewn out of the rock for the purpose. Balthazar looked curiously at the hay-filled manger.

'But this cannot be the place!' he mused to himself, lost in his inner visions, until the others called him to join them in looking for the house of Joseph bar Jacob.

It was Joseph bar Jacob himself who welcomed them into his house. He was a man of substance and proud bearing, though without the haughtiness that they had felt in the presence of Herod. Dismissing his servants, he led them himself into a room where his wife sat in measureless calm, with the child at her breast.

It seemed to Caspar that the woman radiated a deep and penetrating warmth of soul, while Melchior, gazing at the child, felt that here was the source of all the light in the room. Indeed, he felt as though all the light of the world shone from this infant. Balthazar looked at the mother and the child and felt at once joy and sorrow. Compassion welled up in him for the child and His destiny.

The three offered their gifts and spoke prayers of worship and thanksgiving that they had succeeded in their journey. The child seemed to receive their presence in the room, their gifts and prayers with the serenity of the wisdom of ages.

It was already dark when they left the house of Joseph, and went to the inn where their beasts were stabled.

'In the morning,' said Melchior, 'we must return to Herod, and tell him where this child is to be found. Such was his last request to us.'

Balthazar looked out of the window overlooking the little stable, and remained silent.

The massacre of the innocents

In the royal palace, Herod spoke urgently to his Captain of the Guard: 'The foreign priests have told me of the star that they have followed, and this child that they seek could have been born any time in the last two years. Captain, go forth with your best men, and put all the children of that age to death.'

The Captain was dumbfounded. 'All the children two years old or under? All of them?' he asked, his face paling in the lamplight.

'Of course,' said Herod, 'they should not do it for normal wages. They shall be paid extra for this task.'

Before dawn the following day, the three gathered to greet the rising sun. Melchior was the first to speak.

'I dreamed a dream last night,' he said, 'in which I saw the figure of Death at Herod's shoulder.'

'I, too, dreamed,' said Caspar. 'I dreamed of our initiations in the dark corridors, where we learn of evil and suffering of the most dismal kind.'

'I dreamed a dream, too,' replied Balthazar, 'but it was of the Dark Brother of Ahura Mazdao, who I saw whispering in Herod's ear. Ahrimanes himself was inspiring the king to murder and massacre. And indeed, having seen his household, I do believe it.'

'Then we must return to our homes by separate ways, and avoid Herod's company at all costs,' said Melchior, and thus they resolved to part and go home, but not before they expressed to each other the wonder of what they had seen, and how it would live in their souls for all their lives.

†

When the three kingly men had left, Joseph was inspired by his good genius to take his wife and child and leave Bethlehem, their home, as great danger was approaching. As soon as they could, they made their way to Egypt, where they remained with a group of Therapeutae, a group with close affiliations to the Essenes. On the way, the path was beset with dangers and miracles. When they were hungry, a date palm bent its tall trunk to deliver its fruit into their hands. As Herod's soldiers drew near to them in pursuit, they took refuge in a cave, where spiders wove webs across the entrance, so that none would think that anyone could have entered.

At last, Herod died, screaming with fear on his deathbed that he was harnessed to rats, cats and mice, and bound for hellfire. Joseph was still wary of returning home, and again, at the promptings of his higher genius, returned not to Bethlehem, but to Nazareth, in Galilee, where they lived close to an Essene community, and soon made friends there.

As for the three, they made their ways safely home, and returned without incident or mishap. However, Caspar was not to live very long. He was the youngest of the three, and the first to die of a sudden and violent illness, but at the moment of his death, he was looking towards Jerusalem, as though willing his spirit to accompany the child that he had visited in His father's house through His mission on Earth.

Melchior returned to his home and took over the running of his household from the faithful Viligratia. He continued to watch the skies and interpret the meaning of the movements of the stars, but he, too, did not live long.

On the journey home, Balthazar, the oldest of the three, dreamed of the voice of a woman in Ramah, weeping and crying for her murdered children. He knew that the birth of the child had shown Ahura Mazdao's dark brother Ahrimanes the wrathful and cunning that his time was not long, and that at the last, he would be overcome by the child that he, Balthazar, had gone to seek, led by a star.

The pendent boss: Mother and Child to the centre, Kings to the left, Death to the right.

10. Saint Veronica

This is the story of the woman whose story has survived through the ages giving her the name Veronica, which means: 'true countenance'. Other tales were told of this individual, but as always, with legends, the truth disguises itself in a story that survives the passage of time, until the underlying truth can be found again.

Saint Veronica carving, showing the veil with the face of Christ to the right.

The legend of Faustina

Once there was a young woman called Faustina, who was born of parents each of whom suffered from leprosy. In time, she, too, began to feel the disease take hold of her, but she had heard of a great healer and prophet who had the power to cure this sickness. She went to Him, and begged for His help to cure her, and found that a word from Him cleansed her skin and body of the terrible contagion.

Time passed, and it happened that the Emperor Tiberius was stricken by the same foul illness. He forbade all his servants except a trusted few, to come anywhere near him. He would issue his orders to the Captain of the Guard and to his secretary, but kept everyone else at a distance.

The news of this state of affairs reached his old nurse, Faustina, whom he remembered as the only person who would tell him the truth when he was surrounded by hypocrites and toadies, only too willing to encourage him in his decadent excesses. He longed for her presence at this time of his suffering, and eventually, the news came to her in the mountain village where she was staying. She offered to come to him as long as she would not have to see the pomp, arrogance and cruelty that had surrounded him when she was part of his household.

At last, she arrived on the terrace where Tiberius was taking the air, swathed in bandages to cover the extent of his disfigurement. She approached him, and sat beside him on a stool beside the couch where he lay. He at once knew her warm, quiet presence, and asked: 'Faustina, is it truly you?'

She made no answer, but drew his bandaged head to her breast, and, feeling a comfort unknown to him for longer than he could remember, he fell asleep.

Later, they spoke.

'If anyone could cure me of this, you could. But nobody can,' he said.

'There was One who could,' she replied. He shifted uneasily on the couch.

'I should like to see such a person,' he sighed. Faustina rose, and fetched a cloth from her small bundle of belongings. For it was she who, on the path to Golgotha, had offered the Saviour her best cloth to wipe His face of the tears, blood and sweat that covered it. She unrolled it to show the face that remained printed on the fine material. Tiberius looked at the face, and something moved in him.

'This man is truly human,' he said at last. 'We others are animals and beasts; not yet human. But this man is indeed a true Human Being.'

The Emperor was healed, by and by, of his sickness, and the cloth was kept carefully and reverently, as it still bore the image of the countenance of Jesus in the midst of His greatest sufferings. It was known to have miraculous powers of healing, and, over a thousand years later, was a source of inspiration for the Templars, who would incorporate images of the Cloth, or Veil of Veronica in their buildings, with the Countenance of Christ at the centre. Faustina, or she who bears that name in the legend, became known as Veronica, as it was given to her to bear the true countenance of the Christ.

†

That is one of the tales of Saint Veronica; however, she was an historical individual, whose simple, heartfelt act of compassion enraged certain people, and changed the minds of others in an instant. The events described below will be familiar to those who know the Easter story from the Bible or elsewhere. But there are certain people who have a direct and living experience of those events. This has a constant and profound influence on their life and work. One such person is Judith von Halle, whose description of Easter in her book Secrets of the Stations of the Cross *is far more compelling and harrowing than anything given here, but retold in her book with a warm objectivity and deep compassion, as well as a firm and unwavering sense of duty to her destiny as a Christian. With the first part of this story, and the story of Longinus that follows it, we enter a completely different mood from that of the first tale bearing the name of Saint Veronica.*

Saint Veronica: A modern seer's account

The name by which she was known in Jerusalem is lost to us. She was a well-to-do, respectable married woman of about sixty, who kept an inn, a little way to the north of the city, though her house was within the city walls, situated somewhat to the west.

She had developed a connection with the Essenes, and belonged to those who yearned for the coming of the Messiah, the Anointed One. At the funeral of John the Baptist, she was seen to wear a garment torn over the breast to show mourning.

On many occasions, she had welcomed Jesus of Nazareth and His followers into her inn, and recognized in Him a truly great Master. But now, the Master had been arrested, many of His followers had gone into hiding, and there was to be a trial before the Roman Governor, Pontius Pilate at the Feast of Pesach.

The trial took place in the open air, in front of Pilate's house, and in full view of the Forum, where the crowds, made up of people from many nations and all walks of life, jostled for space to see. Between the forum crowd and the accused stood those priests and officials who wished to see judgment brought upon the head of Jesus. A *cordon sanitaire* of darker coloured stones, set into the paving, marked off the area beyond which the priests could not go, for fear of becoming contaminated by the 'impure ones' brought for trial. They were not a quiet and dignified group as they shouted their wishes and instructions to Pilate from their 'hygienic' position, safe from the taint of criminals.

Veronica had no wish to see these proceedings, and kept to her house. Only later did she hear the descriptions of those who witnessed the events leading up to the long, insufferably painful walk to Golgotha.

Jesus had been mercilessly thrashed. His robe, when it was returned to Him after this treatment, was soaked in all manner of foul-smelling filth, the more to humiliate Him. A broad, coarse leather belt was put round His waist, with metal rings to hold the shackles that bound Him before his judges. Two men accused of murder stood on either side of Him; again, to emphasise how low He was being brought.

Pilate, on the judgment seat, knew that he dare not upset the civil authority of Jerusalem, and that this meant that the man before him must be found guilty, even though he could find no fault in the prisoner. Accordingly, he uttered the sentence of death. This pleased his audience of priests and officials, but when he added his justification to the sentence, that he had agreed to the demand for the death penalty to accede to the wishes of the people, and to avoid riot and rebellion in the streets, they shouted their anger. Pilate was shifting the blame for the death of the prisoner on to them, while they had hoped that he would take it upon himself. Furthermore, the document that Pilate signed for the sentence referred to Jesus as 'King of the Jews', to which the High Priests and officials took bitter exception. However, Pilate refused to change it, or any other part of his ruling, and so the sad procession began to make its way out of the city towards Golgotha, the place of execution.

Trumpeters preceded Pilate into his house with all its rich furnishings. As he left the judgment seat, he felt that, in spite of putting his mark on the proceedings by insisting on his own form of words, and refusing to alter any details, he was being led by circumstances; he was not in command of his destiny here in this stony place, so far from the mild climate of his place of birth.*

The shackles were removed from Jesus' wrists, so that He had hands free to carry the great load of timber that was to be the machine of His death. The cross-pieces were strapped to the main upright, and, holding His heavy, drenched and filthy woollen robe in one hand to avoid tripping on its hem, and carrying the wood of the cross over His right shoulder, He was led away.

Ropes were tied to the metal loops on the leather belt, and four soldiers each held an end of each rope, two in front to drag; two behind. A crowd followed, egged on by the Pharisees, who rode their donkeys up and down the procession, shouting encouragement to those who were willing to scream abuse, spit and throw garbage at Him on the way to the hill. The priests, meanwhile, hurried to the Temple, satisfied that their work of condemning a heretic was done, and began to make ready for the Feast of Pesach, the festival of the sacrifice of lambs.

Through the crowded streets they made their way; first the soldiers holding the hammers and nails, ladders, ropes and instruments of torture. After them came a boy with a wooden board, with 'Jesus of Nazareth, King of the Jews' written on it in three languages.

Then came Jesus Himself, bearing His awful burden. A cap, as if a crown woven of long, sharp thorns, had been roughly jammed on to His head, and

---

* There is a legend that Pontius Pilate was born in Fortingall, Perthshire, Scotland, and that he was connected to the Clan Maclaren.

beaten into place with the stick. After Him were the two murderers, each tied to his cross by the cross-pieces.

Veronica heard the noise of the crowd coming ever closer, and busied herself about her work, doing what she could to contain her grief.

A noise went up from the crowd; Jesus had fallen in the street, trying to cross on the stepping-stones across the central drainage channel. The Pharisees exulted. Here was more humiliation, and it was vitally important to them that this man should be brought as low as possible. To see Him in the ditch was a small triumph. The soldiers hauled Him to his feet again after beating Him with their fists. The cap of thorns had fallen off, and it was violently replaced.

The procession turned a corner, and there, hurrying to see what help they could possibly give, were John the disciple, the mother of Jesus, Mary Magdalene, Salome, Martha and the mother of the disciple James. At the sight of these, His strength went out of Him, and he fell for a second time. A stillness fell on the crowd as His mother came and stroked His blood-stained cheek with a gesture that touched the heart of some of the soldiers. However, they had their orders, and these were barked out in plain language. Jesus was hauled to His feet again, and the procession continued.

Jesus fell a third time, dropping the timber of the cross again. Such were His sufferings that his tormentors began to fear that he would die before reaching the hill of execution. A man was dragged from the crowd; one who was just passing. His name was Shimon, and he was a gardener. He was forced to help Jesus to His feet; a task which, taking into account the filth and rubbish sticking to His sopping wet robe, he had no taste for. He resented the imposition on him greatly and even more so when he was required to help to carry the cross.

On they all went again, coming nearer and nearer to Veronica's house. They were going to pass right outside her door. What could she do? She could no longer try to distance herself from this disgraceful, disgusting spectacle of ritual humiliation and those who revelled in it. She went to her door, and saw the procession coming closer. Now, she made up her mind. She would do exactly what she would do under normal circumstances. She would offer Him a handkerchief to wipe His face, and a cup of wine to restore His strength.

She left the doorway and went to fetch these things. But now a thought struck her; instead of a handkerchief, she went to the chest and drew out the finest piece of cloth she had, and draped it over her left shoulder, and carried the wine in her right hand.

Jesus had arrived right outside her door. It was unmistakably her teacher, though beaten, flogged, abused and spat upon. At once, she knew how important it was to do what she had made up her mind to do. In spite of the violent mob, ignoring the soldiers and ignoring the power and influence of the Pharisees, she went out and knelt before Him, and offered Him the cloth. He took it and wiped His face with it, leaving the imprint of His face in blood and sweat on the fine cloth. He even tried to fold it, so that in handing it back to her, it would be clean side uppermost. The mob, for a moment, became quiet. This gesture of respect and veneration was unexpected, and had its own power among the crowd watching. She then offered Him the wine, but the spell was broken, and the soldiers pushed her away, not allowing Jesus any of it.

The Pharisees were furious. Their aim was to see this man rendered as low as the dogs, and yet, here was a woman who showed Him reverence, who knelt before Him, who treated Him as though He were a person worthy of respect. They rode their asses back and forth hurling curses at her, and admonishing the crowd not to follow her example.

But it was too late. Some had seen what had happened, and were touched by it. Among those was Shimon the gardener, known to history as Simon of Cyrene, who felt his disgust for the task and for the prisoner change to a deep compassion. All the way to the place of execution, he did what he could to make it easier for the prisoner, though that was precious little.

Jesus fell three more times before reaching the top of the hill, and at last, He fell for the last time, at which the soldiers took advantage of His prone position to put the pieces of the cross together and to nail Him to the timber.

And so the purpose of the High Priests and the officials and the Pharisees was achieved. What they could not guess was that, at the same time, Jesus Christ's mission in the world was accomplished.

Veronica experienced the darkness that spread over the earth, and heard what she took to be the rumblings of earthquakes in the next days. She was told that the veil of the Temple, hiding the Holy of Holies was torn by no human agency. She also learned, some time later, that He had been seen since the crucifixion; that He had walked and talked with the disciples. Her humility was such that only gradually did she realize the significance of her act of love and compassion for a revered teacher. But then, as she said to herself on occasion, what else could she possibly have done? She quite

The carving usually known as the Crown of Thorns.

*Carving said by some to be the 'true' Crown of Thorns; shown to be more
cap-like than wreath-shaped.*

simply could not have acted otherwise, for love was what she had learned from her teacher.

It is that love for which she is honoured in Christian churches all over the world; it is the reason why the Templars held her in particular veneration, and why she is remembered in Rosslyn.

11. The Soldiers of Golgotha

It was only much later in the chapel's history that the stained-glass windows were added to Rosslyn. The Rev John Thompson mentions the windows in the main body of the chapel in his guide, but he does not make note of the pair of windows that depict two military men whose lives foreshadow the ideals of the Knights Templar in their relationship to Christ and the world. It is certain that these windows were commissioned by someone with a deep connection to the ideas and ideals of William Sinclair, Third Earl of Orkney.

One of the men represented in this pair of windows is Cassius Longinus. In this man we see something of the spirit that the Templar Knights tried to incorporate into their Order, and into themselves; a willingness to follow an intuition on behalf of a greater good, and the taking of a vow so sacred that it was dearer than life itself. We know hardly anything about Longinus, yet he had an important role to play in the central event of Christianity, the Crucifixion on the hill of Golgotha. We include the story of Abn Adar here as the story of Longinus is incomplete without the contribution of this other soldier to the scene.

Abn Adar

In our recounting of the story of Saint Veronica, we followed the agonizing path of Jesus to Golgotha, and His collapse at the crown of the hill. At this, the soldiers immediately executed their orders, and nailed Him to the cross that He had carried so painfully, aided by Simon of Cyrene, whose compassion for Jesus in this extremity of human cruelty was to change his life. Simon had wished to stay to see what further tortures this man was to be put through, but he was turned roughly away, having done what he was ordered.

Two others were crucified at the same time; murderers whose ignominious death was supposed to make that of Jesus all the more dishonourable in the eyes of the Pharisees. One of these was crucified facing the north-east, away from the sun, while the other found his last moments illuminated by the midday sun, before the sky darkened, as the Gospels relate. This was he who refused to join in the mockery that his fellow criminal indulged in.

The captain in charge of the soldiers sent to Golgotha was one Abn Adar, a man of Arab antecedents, in charge at this point of about fifty men. Part of his work was to see the execution carried out, according to orders; part of it was to police the crowd that gathered to watch. Many of these were shouting abuse or mockery, including the murderer to the left of Jesus. Neither he nor his brother in crime had been nailed to their crosses, but tied with ropes.

Just as Jesus had fallen seven times on His way to Golgotha, He spoke seven times on the cross before giving up the ghost, and the first of His words was to forgive those who mocked and abused Him.

The second word that Jesus spoke was to His mother, and to John, the disciple whom He loved. To His mother He said: 'Woman, behold your son.' To John, He said: 'Behold your mother.' Even amid His agony, He was achieving what He had come to fulfil. Blood relationships were no longer to be the limit of love and compassion, but all men and women were to endeavour to love one another.

The sky was growing dark and the noise of the crowd was growing. The murderer to the left of Jesus, he who faced away from the sun, joined in the mocking, shrieking at Jesus to get down from the cross. Even as he did so, the other murderer felt an inner transformation beyond the pain of his suffering, and he recognized in Jesus the Son of the Living God.

To him, Jesus spoke the third word: 'Truly I say to you, you will be with me in Paradise this day.'

As the day wore on, the skies grew dark; earthquakes shook the countryside around. Chaos and confusion spread through the crowd, and there was panic in the streets of Jerusalem. Angry mobs turned on Pontius Pilate, blaming him for the death of the man whose execution many of them had angrily demanded earlier. Pilate now wanted as little more to do with this episode as possible, and when Joseph of Arimathea, who had watched the crucifixion from a little distance from Golgotha, came to ask for the body, Pilate granted permission at once, partly in the hope of pleasing the gods whom he had angered by his judgment, and partly to spite the Pharisees.

Abn Adar, his spirit stirred to its depths by what he had seen on the hill of execution, and the strange darkening of the sky and the earthquake, refused to allow any more shouting of abuse or mockery.

The fourth word that Jesus spoke is recorded in the Gospel as: 'My God, my God, why hast Thou forsaken me?'

The fifth word that Jesus spoke was: 'I thirst.' This caused ever greater pain to those close to Him who were present, as none of them had anything to give Him to slake this terrible thirst. Abn Adar pushed a cloth soaked in vinegar on to the end of a pole, and reached it up to Jesus, who accepted this bitter drink.

Such was the effect on Abn Adar, hearing the last words that he proclaimed Jesus as the Living God, and refused to carry out any further orders.

Jesus spoke twice more before He died. The sixth word was: 'It is finished.' Finally, He said: 'Into thy hands, Father, I commend my spirit.'

Gaius Cassius Longinus

Meanwhile, even some Pharisees were now changing their minds. Shouts of mockery and abuse were being replaced by cries of terror and wailing. Others were leaving the city to see what was happening. Pilate now ordered hundreds of soldiers out to keep the peace. Now that Abn Adar had resigned his post, however, a new officer had to be found quickly to take his place.

A young man called Gaius Cassius Longinus was promoted to the position vacated so hastily by Abn Adar, and he rode up to the hill. As he did so, men of the Temple Guard were sent to break the bones of the crucified men, to hasten their deaths. Those close to Jesus did all they could to prevent this, and indeed, a prophecy had stated: 'A bone of him shall not be broken.' The men with cudgels whose job it was to break the bones of the crucified, left Jesus' body alone, and went about their task with the other two.

The sight of the Temple Guards beating and cudgelling the heads and limbs of the two murderers filled Cassius with disgust. To him it appeared that Jesus was still living, though life had departed some little time since. Seized by a sudden intuition, the origin of which he could neither explain nor justify, he rode quickly up the hill, and, standing before the cross upon which the Saviour hung, he drove his spear between Jesus' fourth and fifth ribs on the right side, and blood flowed from the corpse into a shallow depression at the foot of the cross. In this moment, Cassius Longinus, too, proclaimed Jesus the Son of the Living God. An old legend tells further that he had been suffering from failing eyesight, and that in this moment, his sight was restored.

12. The Cockle Shell

The early chronicler of Rosslyn, Father Hay, records that William Sinclair, third Earl of Orkney, feeling 'his age creeping on him, made him consider how he had spent his time past, and how to spend that which was to come.' According to Father Hay, Earl William built Rosslyn in order that prayers might be said for him for as long as the chapel lasted. The overwhelming sense is that Earl William was thinking of his spiritual self, rather than his temporal self. Of course, it should be clear by this point that anxiety for his immortal soul was not by any means the sole reason for Sinclair's decision to build Rosslyn.

A carving in the north-east of the chapel shows the face of one who is awakened to the reality of death, and the fear of what might follow. Above the awakened face is the Recording Angel, and on diagonal ribs close by, the Dance of Death is depicted: the figure of Death dancing with representatives from all walks of medieval life. The implication is clear. In the words of the Scottish medieval poet William Dunbar in his Lament for the Makars: Timor mortis conturbat me, the fear of death disturbs me.

Earl William could have Rosslyn built, but for poorer persons, it was possible to expiate one's sins by going on a pilgrimage. The most common destination was Compostela, in Spain, once the Holy Land was closed to Christian pilgrims, and those who made the pilgrimage to the Shrine of Saint James at Compostela would bring a cockle shell back with them as a sign that they had been successful in their quest.

These shells would be ground into the mortar that holds the chapel together to this day. Rosslyn, then, is held together by the piety of those early pilgrims.

James the son of Zebedee

The cockle shell is the symbol of Saint James, son of Zebedee and of Salome. He and his brother John were the first to be chosen by Christ as His disciples, along with Simon Peter and his brother Andrew. We see in the story of the Templars, how James was associated in their initiation ceremonies with the element of water, and indeed, when he was chosen to follow Christ, James earned his livelihood as a fisherman, going out on to the water to make his living. Indeed, Jesus found James at the task of

casting his net on the waters on the Sea of Galilee, near the town of Bethsaida. The name of the town, or village, means 'the House of Fish'. Nothing of it remains today, but the site where it stood has the Arabic name *Tabgha,* which in turn derives from the Greek name *Heptapegon,* the place of seven springs. Several springs do, in fact rise in the surrounding hills, and each brings with it down to the waters of Galilee different mineral properties, some of which attract fish and therefore make for rewarding fishing.

We can imagine James, in his boat on the waters of Galilee, with the fertile land all around, being summoned among the first disciples. Some others who followed Jesus came from the same area. Philip was from Bethsaida, and Matthew, the Gospel writer and patron saint of Rosslyn, was stationed there when he was an exciseman, or customs official. The countryside differs strongly from the rocky, arid land of Judea.

James was later chosen, along with John and Peter to witness one of the most mysterious events in the life of Christ, the Transfiguration on Mount Tabor. It was not given to all the disciples to witness this happening, when Jesus conversed with Moses and Elijah, surrounded by a cloud of spirit-light. This marked an important step in the development of Jesus' mission, and could only be shared with those who were awakened enough inwardly to perceive it, even if they could not yet understand it.

After that, the story of Jesus unfolded to its end — at least, in the earthly sphere. The Crucifixion took place, and what seemed the death of all hope. But then came the Resurrection and a new understanding of the meaning of Christ's mission on Earth among humanity.

After the Ascension, when Christ at last returned to the heavens, though with the promise of His return, James journeyed abroad to preach the Gospel of Christ, and he travelled as far as Spain. In the year 40 ad, he had a vision of the Mother of Jesus, calling him back to Judea. James set off on a long and arduous journey that took him through desert wastes, where thirst was one of the greatest hazards. However, the thought that Christ was always with him on his journey sustained him through the longest, most arid miles of his path, and thus he took the cockle shell as a symbol of water in the desert.

When he finally arrived in Judea, he made his way to the tomb where Christ arose after three days, and he worshipped there, as he had promised the Mother of Jesus when he had first had his vision.

The news that one of the disciples of Jesus of Nazareth had returned and was worshipping at the tomb and preaching the Gospel came to the ears of the King, Herod Antipas. Such was his rage at the Christians that he is said to have beheaded James himself, with his sword. Thus James was the first Christian martyr.

His remains were taken by some of the remaining disciples by ship to Spain, and after being lost for centuries, were revealed in a field by stars shining overhead; hence the name Compostela: 'The Field of Stars'. These remains became the basis of the shrine that bears his name, and the end of a pilgrimage trail that is still followed to this day. The cockle shell is the symbol of this pilgrimage.

The Knight of the Cockle

Two of the uncles of Rosslyn's founder, Earl William, visited the shrine of Saint James of Compostela on their ill-fated journey to place the heart of Robert the Bruce in the soil of the Holy Land, in Jerusalem, and, according to Rosslyn expert and guide Fiona Scott, William Sinclair also made the pilgrimage, bringing back a cockle shell as the sign that he had done so. As we have seen, Compostela means 'field of stars', and the star-studded ceiling over the western end of the chapel is said to be, among the other things that it symbolizes, a reminder of the connection with the shrine of Saint James.

However, the symbolism of the cockle shell goes some way further. The painters of the Renaissance used symbolism in ways that we are less able to read now without a specialist education. The great artist of the Renaissance, Botticelli, painted *The Birth of Venus* in the year following the death of Earl William Sinclair. The earl could never have seen it, but he would have understood the placing of the chaste and beautiful Venus on a cockle shell as the vessel on which she arrives, blown by friendly Zephyrus to dwell among human beings, all in a shower of roses, and greeted by nymphs who seek to maintain her modesty with a purple cloak. Venus in this painting represents all that is most revered in the feminine, understood in those times as the bringer and nurturer of life. She appears unveiled in the picture, and with the serenity of her countenance touched with just a hint of melancholy. We can see in this painting a glimpse of the future; Isis unveiled.

William Sinclair, founder of Rosslyn, was also a Knight of the Cockle. This was an order of no more than thirteen men, and Sinclair was received among this exclusive brotherhood in 1431. We recall that the most highly initiated of the Templars also numbered no more than thirteen. The Order of the Cockle understood the most noble aims of the Templars, and strove to honour them, but without what one might call the spiritual impatience of the Templars to raise the material substance of the Earth into spirit, through their own inner transformation: their single-minded pursuit of the Grail.

We know also that at the heart of the Templars' spirituality was a deep reverence for the feminine. William Sinclair, Knight of the Cockle, honoured this in Rosslyn through the many carvings that show female figures: the Mother of Jesus, Saint Veronica, Saint Margaret, the Mother and Child turning away from the devil, as depicted in the north-west window. The small, red window, high in the Eastern wall, which is illuminated at each equinox with the rays of the rising sun, and casts a circle of warm, red light on the opposite wall, is a sign in the chapel that recalls the Shekinah: the feminine aspect of the Divine, who took pity on Adam and Eve when they were cast out of Paradise, and promised to follow them and their children through time. The cockle shell, then, is the vessel that supports the feminine, as represented in Botticelli's painting, but also in the mortar that binds the structure of Rosslyn together, so that the chapel can honour and support the feminine principle, in a way that the Templars would have wished.

Saint James was, for the Templars, the representative of the forces of life symbolically represented by water; the element that we have in common with plants and the animal kingdom. The cockle shell is hard and stone-like substance, but clearly and beautifully formed. It is no accident that in many churches cockle shells are used to scoop up the water from the font to sprinkle on the infant being baptized. Life, the water, and form, the cockle shell, come together in this ceremony, where the life of the child is finding the physical human form.

The cockle shell is also the thing that symbolically bears the feminine, bringer and nurturer of life. Once we see how far the feminine is revered in the chapel, and the deep regard for the life forces of the world characterized by the multifarious carvings of plant life, we see that Rosslyn itself is a sort of cockle shell, cradling its treasures on the edge of the brae overlooking Roslin Glen.

William Sinclair, founder of Rosslyn, with the cockle shell motif visible just below him.

13. Mani and the Cathars

Cathars, Bogomils, Patarenes, Albigensians: these are some of the names given to the followers of a remarkable spiritual teacher who lived in the third century ad, and whose influence was felt from Spain to China, before being savagely put down by various enemies, including, at last, the Church. Nevertheless, Mani's teachings flourished for about a thousand years before they were subject to the wrath of their enemies.

There are several carvings in Rosslyn that are connected to Mani. First, there is the architrave which on one side shows the seven cardinal virtues, and on the other, the seven deadly sins; there is a carving in the westernmost window in the north wall that shows a demonic figure holding the hem of the garments of a mother and child who resolutely turn away from him to face the long-stemmed cross held by an angel in the opposite corner, and there are details in the ceiling at the westernmost end of the chapel, which on the north side show the Fourth Heaven of the Cathars, including the sun at midnight, or spiritual sun, crescent moon and five-pointed stars, as well as the Dove with an olive branch; while on the south side, there are depicted the four Archangels of the seasons, with one raising his hands in the orant, or praying gesture of the Cathars.

But before we discuss how these elements relate to Mani and his followers, let us consider his story.

The life of Mani

In the year 216 ad, on April 14, in the city of Seleucia-Ctesiphon, on the banks of the River Tigris, in Mesopotamia, a boy was born to a righteous man by the name of Fatak of the family Kurkabios. He was a pious and upright member of the sect known as the Elchasaites, a baptizing sect of Gnostics who were devotees of the teachings that were given in the name of the Hidden Power, or El-Chasai. Their way of life was austere and with few creature comforts.

The boy Shuraiq was brought up by his mother at first, as his father's commitment to his sect demanded that he live with them. She was a righteous woman, connected to the royal family of Parthia, and she was a Marcionite Christian. This group rejected the Old Testament and Jehovah, whom they took to be a jealous and violent god. When Shuraiq reached the age of four however, Fatak sent for him, and he became a member of the same community as his father. The pious example of Fatak soon impressed itself on his son.

At the age of twelve, Shuraiq had a deep, intensely profound mystical experience. He referred to it as the meeting with his higher self, or 'twin' — *al-Taum* in his own language. Through this spiritual awakening, Shuraiq learned of the destiny that he was to fulfil.

In his early twenties, he had a further vision, which he communicated to the people of the El-Chasai sect, but he was disappointed in their response. He inaugurated a centre through which he began to propagate his own teachings through Mesopotamia and Persia, but he left this in the year 241 ad to go travelling through the East, visiting the religious centres and mystery temples.

On his return, a new king was on the throne of Persia, Shapur I. Shuraiq had now adopted the name Mani, which is to say Manas-bearer (see also Chapter 4). That is to say: he had incorporated into his being the *Manas,* a higher aspect of the human soul. He was able to meet Shapur. The Persian king was highly impressed by Mani's depth of wisdom and the quality of his teachings, and became a convert to his way of religious life. This was a blow to the Zoroastrian priests, who, up until that moment, had enjoyed the royal patronage, but was keen to maintain the support that they were in the habit of receiving. Mani recognized many teachers before him, including Seth, Enosh, Enoch, Shem, Zarathustra and Buddha, making it clear that he valued them all as true servants of Christ. The teachings of Paul were highly regarded by him, too.

Mani and his disciples became ever more popular in Persia. They travelled widely in the kingdom and established many communities. Mani himself showed himself to be a first-rate organizer, as well as a man of prodigious literary talent, but in order to couch his message in language and terminology that satisfied him, he had to re-invent a form of writing in the Iranian language through which his teachings could be spread. This he did, not once but twice; and the Syriac language is still the richer for Mani's literary achievement. His books, according to accounts of the time, were beautifully written and illustrated, though sadly none of his originals have survived. His disciples were able to follow his lead and write down copies of his most important works.

It was when Mani was well-established in his mission that he began to refer to himself as the Son of the Widow, looking forward to a period when people would no longer look for authority from outwith themselves, but search within their souls for direction from the inner light of spirit: the Osiris-light as sought by his widowed spouse Isis.

Mani's followers were divided into two groups: the Elect, a very few who had received and understood Mani's teaching, and the Hearers, those who would listen to the teachings, but ask no questions. When such a person was deemed worthy by the Elect, he could be received into their company. This will seem a highly élitist structure, and no doubt it was. However, it took no account of secular caste or social hierarchical conditions, and rather subverted them. The Elect could contain those who were not very elevated socially, and the Hearers could number kings and princes among them.

In about 255 AD, Mani set out eastwards again, travelling through Khorasan to Turkestan. Here he spent a year living in a cave, spending his time in meditation and living on the food that the surroundings afforded him. He took no meat but survived on a diet of herbs, roots and berries. The cave walls were covered in paintings at the end of the year, the results of his spiritual vision. He then continued eastwards into China, where he founded new communities of followers which lasted until they were savagely put down by the Mongol advances of the thirteenth century.

Mani returned to Persia by way of Tibet and Kashmir. He learned on his return that Shapur had died, but his son Hormuzd was now on the throne and Hormuzd was a disciple of Mani. However, this friendly king died within the year, and was succeeded by Bahram, who was a staunch supporter of the Zoroastrian priesthood, who had felt so usurped by Mani when he gained the enthusiastic approval of King Shapur.

Mani was known as a healer, and when a royal prince fell ill, Mani was called upon to heal him. Sadly, all his ministrations failed. When the prince died, it went hard with Mani and he was banished from the court. Some time later, he appealed to Bahram for reinstatement, but this failed, largely owing to the interference of the Zoroastrian priest Karter. Mani now found himself thrown into prison in the city of Jundishapur.

His trial was notable for Mani's clarity of defence, Bahram's stubborn refusal to accept his testimony and the treachery of Karter. Mani was sentenced to death.

The method of execution was a particularly cruel one: he was to be flayed alive, and his skin stuffed with straw and hung above one of the city gates, known from that time afterwards as The Mani Gate. This method of execution could be the source of the accusation against the Templar Knights that they worshipped a flayed human skin stuffed with straw, and basted with the fat of roasted children; it was well-known that the Templars held the teachings of Mani in the greatest reverence.

Groups who followed his teachings covered a wide area, from Spain to China, though the names they took differed from place to place, and the emphasis they placed on their devotion to Mani differed according to the spiritual constitution of the place; thus in the East, there was a great interest in the stories that Mani told, of the creation of the world and other matters. In the West, the 'scientific' aspects of his descriptions appealed to people, as well as the asceticism that he embraced.

At roughly the same time as the Mongol armies were stamping out Mani's heritage in the East, the Church was following a similarly savage campaign against Mani's followers in the Languedoc region of what is now south-west France. This was known as the Albigensian Crusade, and resulted in thousands of people being burnt alive for the sin of heresy.

Why were Mani's teachings judged to be heretical? After all, here was a man who taught a Christian doctrine of peace and light. The answer lies in the difference between his direct spiritual perceptions and the dogma of the Church. The Catholic Church understood Mani to teach that the world was the creation of the Devil; that Good and Evil were eternally in balance with one another and that Good could never entirely prevail.

This was a mistaken idea, as we shall see. For one thing, Mani distinguished not between Good and Evil, but between Darkness and Light.

This may seem a quibble, but it points to an entirely different quality in understanding of the spirit than his enemies in the Church showed. His teachings are sometimes known as the Religion of Light. The Church also believed that Mani denied the Crucifixion and Resurrection. They were on firmer ground here. When Mani looked into the stream of time and saw the record of human history in the life energies of the world-all, he felt the power of the Comforter, the Holy Spirit; he experienced the Risen Christ, walking and talking with the Disciples in the period between Easter and Ascension. He knew that it was impossible to put such a Being to death. He saw Christ as Jesus the Radiant, accompanying humanity from first beginnings in the spirit, awakening and teaching Adam.

He taught that the world exists in the tension between Light and Dark, and that the work of transformation for mankind has as its aim the freeing of the Light that was captured before the world began by demonic beings. The physical world is made up of Light and Dark mixed, and to be born into the flesh is to be swallowed by the Dragon, but our task is to transform the Dragon from within. This is a long and arduous process, and as long as we are in a body of flesh, even the most innocent of us finds that the Devil has hold of the hem of our garments; that is, has some power over us. By the same token, even the worst of us has a spark of the Divine Light as the source of a chance of redemption.

Mani also taught that we are reincarnated, which was another bone of contention between the Church's teachings and his own, as the Church had decided no longer to teach reincarnation in the early years of its existence, as the thought that we might have a second chance at the path of redemption could lead to dangerous moral complacency. Mani taught that the Buddha and Zarathustra were servants of the Father of Greatness, the Most High God, which also went against the grain of orthodox Christian teaching, which tended to write off the earlier great teachers as pagan, foreign to the Christian spirit, and irrelevant, if not dangerously misleading. But the influence of Mani was widespread, and inspired, among other things, the ideal of the San Greal, or Holy Grail, revered by various groups united by a form of chivalry in the Arthurian sense, and especially the Knights Templar, who were admirers of Mani, and brought some of his practices into their own initiation rituals.

Mani's story of Creation

In the beginning there were two realms; that of Light and that of Darkness. These were the two Great Roots. The realm of Light was the abode of the Father of Greatness, and there all was beautiful, peaceful and harmonious. It was the place of the five bright dwellings: Sense, Reason, Thought, Imagination and Intention. The other realm was one of chaos, stink, noise, enmity and confusion. There was suffocating smoke, poisonous water, destructive fire and darkness you could feel. In the beginning, these realms were separate. This was the First Great Moment: the Past.

Now, the lord of the region of darkness caught a scent of the realm of Light, and knew that he wished to possess it, and so he gathered his demons about him to invade. However, the Father of Greatness grew aware of the coming invasion, and took steps to counteract it. We can ask ourselves: how does a Being that is entirely good meet an attack of this nature, without sacrificing His own goodness?

He called into being the Mother of Life, who in turn called into being the Primal Man. The Primal Man was sent, preceded by the angel Nahashbat, bearing a crown of victory, equipped with the five bright essences, to meet the invasion of the forces of the Dark. The Five Bright Essences are the essences of fire, water, wind, light and ether. The dark Archons snatched these away and devoured them. Thus the Five Bright Essences became mingled with the substance of the demons of the dark, and their nature began to be changed. They were no longer entirely dark.

The Primal Man was left prostrate in the place where he had met the Archons of the Dark, but now three more mighty beings were called into existence by the Father of Greatness, and these were the Beloved of the Lights, the Great Ban and the Living Spirit. They restored the Primal Man to his former strength, and he at once descended into the deepest abyss of the realm of the Dark, and cut the roots of the tree of Death, such that it could never increase. The Great Ban was the architect who made sure that the realm of Darkness was firmly limited within strong boundaries. Thus Mani taught that, ultimately, the powers of the dark Archons were never of equal power to those of the Father of Greatness. Those Archons that had devoured the light essences were forced to give back what they could of the stolen light, and the Beloved of the Lights made of this disgorged light essence the Sun and the Moon. The sky and the Earth were formed of the dark Archons, and the mountains raised high, so that the light could continue to be distilled from the substance of the darkness in dew.

The World took its place in the Cosmos, with Splenditenens holding the cosmos suspended like a bright chandelier; the King of Honour collecting in the rays of light from his being the distilled fragments of light particles; Adamant, who guards the world with his spear from further incursions from the realm of Darkness; together with the King of Glory, who revolves the cosmic spheres; and Atlas, who supports the heavens on his shoulders. These five great ones the Father of Greatness called forth. Each took up their place.

Then He spoke, and the Messenger came forward. The Messenger went down to the Archons of the Dark and appeared beautiful to them, so that they poured forth their captured light to woo him. The Messenger then set about separating the light from the substance with which it had been mixed. Where this substance fell into the ocean, it became a great serpent, in the image of the King of the Archons, and Adamant transfixed it with his spear. Where it fell on to the land, it became the plants and animals. The light freed by the Messenger was placed in the Sun and Moon.

The Lord of the Archons now called to him his spouse, and they devoured those Archons in whom remained some of the bright essences. He then fathered on his consort Adam and Eve, beings who contained the last of the bright essences taken from the Primal Man, beings, moreover, made in the image of the Messenger.

Adam and Eve were set sleeping on the ground, with a guard of Archons around them. But there now came to them Jesus the Living Spirit, the Friend, who chased away the archon guards and awoke the slumbering Adam. Jesus the Radiant showed Adam a glimpse of the heavenly hierarchies, and explained to him how he had come to be. Adam bitterly mourned the Darkness that was part of his nature, but resolved to begin the work of transformation, so that Light and Dark should once again be in their rightful places, but with this difference: that in due course human beings could take their place beside the angels.

Thus began the second Great Moment, 'the Present'. 'The Future' will come about when the world is transformed through human effort of all kinds, from the tilling of the soil to the building of the Temple.

Mani was put to death in the year 277. The date was February 26. A thousand years later, his followers throughout the world were harried and hunted out of existence or into hiding. However, Mani's teachings managed to survive. Some of them were taken up by the Templar Knights, and even when the Templars were destroyed, there were groups who continued to live in the way that Mani taught. Among these was the 'Family of Love' that existed in Holland in the sixteenth century, and to whom it is thought the painter Hieronymus Bosch belonged. Mani the artist continued to inspire artists.

Mani's world and Rosslyn Chapel

His picture of the Heavens and the Earth was as follows: the Highest Heaven, the Seventh Heaven, was the abode of the Father of Greatness, God the Father. Below Him was the Sixth Heaven, the dwelling place of the Higher Angels. The Fifth Heaven was the home of the High Angels, and below them was the Fourth Heaven, where the Spiritual Sun, the Sun at Midnight, ever shines, beside the Spiritual Moon and Stars. In the realm below the Fourth Heaven is to be found the Tree of Life and the Fountain of Life, from which flow the four streams that water our own physical world below. This is also known as the Place of Transformation, the threshold between Creator and Created; a realm of ever changing and everlasting potential.

The Second Heaven belongs to the Lesser Angels, but the First Heaven, just beyond our own world of matter mixed with spirit, is the First Heaven, where Satan has his throne.

Now we come to the created world, framed by the Firmament, where we share our dwelling with fallen angels. It is a place of discord. Below our world are the Waters under the Earth.

This is shown in a beautiful way in the carvings in the chapel. The vaulted ceiling in the west shows the Sun at Midnight, Moon and Stars on the north side, and facing it, in the south, four Archangels of the Seasons face the Spiritual Sun, Moon and Stars. Michael, with drawn sword is placed highest, as befits the archangelic patron of the Templar Knights. Below Him, a little to the left, Raphael raises his arms in the distinctive orant, or praying, gesture of the Cathars. Two more Archangels are placed below the first two. A little above the Crescent Moon we see a dove, with olive branch in its beak. This is the universal symbol of the Holy Spirit, but birds were for the Cathars and other followers of Mani, symbolic of the spiritual human being.

The Apprentice Pillar is a representation of the Tree of Life. All the carved plant imagery in Rosslyn starts with the Apprentice Pillar, and spreads out continuously across the chapel, so that both the Fourth Heaven and the Third Heaven are clearly shown in the structure of Rosslyn. At the base of the Apprentice Pillar we see dragons gnawing the roots, showing, once again, the tension between Dark and Light in which we live.

Below the western part of the ceiling is the window where mother and child turn towards the long-stemmed cross in the arms of an angel, while a demon has tight hold of the hem of their garments. This is very clearly a Manichean picture. There is also in this connection the architrave in the south aisle that shows the Seven Cardinal Virtues on one side, and the Seven Deadly Sins on the other. However, when we examine the Cardinal Virtues, we find Greed among them, as though one can be greedy for the spirit, and forget the needs of one's fellow man, and the burdens that we all carry, no matter how virtuous. On the other side, that most Christian virtue of Charity is found among the sinners — swallowed, as it were, by the Dragon of sin, to transform it from within. Rosslyn, then, among its other treasures, is rich in Manichean imagery.

Dragons gnawing the roots of the Tree of Life at the base of the Apprentice Pillar.

Demon holding the hem of the garments of the innocents.

14. The Twin Dragons

The carving of the twin dragons is to be seen on the interior west wall, reminding us first of those dragons at the base of the Apprentice Pillar, which we have identified as part of the Manichean aspect of Rosslyn. Yet dragons are not always harbingers of evil. Some of the experts who have examined Rosslyn's carvings identify a Chinese influence in the dragons at the base of the Apprentice Pillar, for instance, and the Chinese respect for the dragon is well-known. The dragon in Chinese mythology is one of the Four Propitious Creatures who assisted the godlike being Pan-Ku as he created the material world.

In a Christian setting we cannot help but remember the Dragon of the Apocalypse of Saint John, whose influence is kept within bounds by Saint Michael. The dragons on the wall in Rosslyn, though, are peaceful creatures. The question is: why are they there? To answer that, we must look into the central myth of Britain, that of King Arthur.

The mountain Arthur's Seat, named for the Celtic warrior hero so glorified in medieval romance, sits in the midst of the city of Edinburgh, surrounded by rocky crags and cliffs, in the Queen's Park. The first mention of Arthur in literature occurs in a work called The Gododdin, *by a writer known only as Aneurin. The Gododdin were a Brythonic tribe who lived in the Edinburgh region, and we are told that one of their heroes was a great warrior, 'though he was no Arthur'. This fleeting and slight reference is the first in which the great leader of the Dark Ages is named, but it shows that Arthur was known as a great hero in Scotland; in fact,*

Alistair Moffat argues forcibly in his book Arthur and the Lost Kingdoms *that Arthur was a Scottish hero, and Camelot was in Scotland, though he is still claimed by the descendants of the Brythonic people, the Welsh and Cornish, as their own. But once, the land of the Britons stretched from Cornwall to the Firth of Forth and the Clyde Valley. The story opens with Vortigern, the leader who usurped the place of Arthur's father, Uther Pendragon. His real name is lost in infamy; Vortigern is simply an old Celtic term meaning 'Great Chief'.*

Vortigern and the Saxon princes

Vortigern, King of the Britons, was growing desperate as his enemies were growing stronger and more numerous. He hoped that in the mountains of Snowdonia, he could hold out against those who sought his overthrow and death. Therefore, he ordered the construction of an impregnable fortress wherein he could outlast any siege, and from it ride out to confound and destroy his enemies. The construction work began in the high mountains, but soon the builders found that when they came to work in the mornings, the previous day's work lay all in ruins, and they had it all to do again.

When the last of the Roman legions left Britain, he intrigued and plotted his way to the leadership, and had not stopped at murder. But now men from beyond the Forth and Clyde valleys and from Ireland were attacking his lands, and he did not have the military strength to meet them.

He had invited two Saxon leaders, Hengist and Horsa, to come with their armies to help fight the incursions from the north and west, and in return he would reward them with rich lands within Britain to settle as their own.

He met the Saxon warriors on the Kentish coast, and marvelled at the dragon-headed longships in which they had travelled the cold North Sea.

'Welcome, welcome in Christ's name,' Vortigern cried, spreading his arms to receive them.

The Saxon princes, Hengist and Horsa, looked at Vortigern with clear, blue eyes.

'Thanks for your welcome, King of the Britons,' said Hengist, 'but we worship the god Odin, whom you know as Mercury. He it was who gave us safe passage over the waves.'

As he spoke, his eyes seemed to take in immense distances. Horsa, on the other hand, looked shrewdly at the land that lay before them, assessing its worth, and finding it good. He spoke never a word. A cold feeling spread through Vortigern as he realized that there was far less common ground between his potential allies and himself than he had hoped. The men who had accompanied the princes were battle-hardened soldiers. Already, standing on the wind-scoured beach, Vortigern had begun doubt the wisdom of inviting them to fight on his behalf.

The Saxon leaders agreed to help however, and their strength and determination in meeting the attacks from the Picts and Scots was considerable. But the land that they had been offered was indeed rich, and they wanted more. Soon, Vortigern found it necessary to fight his erstwhile allies, while those who had been dispossessed to pay the Saxons were angry, and in arms against him.

Now, he stood among the ruins of the fortress that he relied upon to be his stronghold and source of power. Great stones and wooden beams lay tumbled all about, as though brought down by an avalanche.

At last, Vortigern summoned his advisers and counsellors, and demanded to be clearly informed why the structures would not stand.

'The foundation land needs a sacrifice, O King,' he was told.

'Very well then; take a ram from the flocks and sacrifice it.'

'This needs more than the blood of a ram,' they told him. Vortigern pondered. He was loath to sacrifice a stallion, but if that was what the work needed, so be it.

'No stallion, no, not even the best of your stable, can pay the blood price here,' they told him. Vortigern then understood that they were looking for a human sacrifice; for human blood to be spilled on the ground of the foundations so that the work could continue.

'Find your sacrifice and make ready,' he ordered.

Now there was a lad living in the south of the country whose mother was a princess of the Demetian people, though she now lived as a holy anchorite in a convent near the sea. As a young girl she had a child born out of wedlock, and the tale she told was that Lucifer himself had come to her, in spite of all locks and bars on the doors and tight-closed shutters on the windows. He had lain with her, and the fruit of that union was this boy named Myrddin, or Merlin, who was now a youth. He sought no company, but loved to wander in the forests, where he could commune with the nature spirits and know their secrets.

Merlin was seized and brought in chains to Vortigern's camp, where the construction was progressing no further.

'Who is this?' demanded the King.

'This is the boy born of a human woman and the devil. His blood will make the foundations sure,' said the advisers. Merlin looked at the old men, and could see that their understanding was dim. He laughed out loud at their pretensions to knowledge and wisdom.

'Why do you laugh?' asked Vortigern. 'There is little for you to find funny here.'

'I laugh at these old fools! They think my blood will save the work? It will make no difference at all.'

The look in Merlin's eyes, his proud stance and complete lack of fear in the face of imminent death impressed Vortigern.

'Perhaps you can tell us more than they can of the reasons why the work is destroyed daily?' he asked. Merlin smiled, and Vortigern began to grow angry.

'Answer or die!' he commanded. Merlin looked at him steadily.

'Tell your men to dig down below the foundations,' he said. 'They shall find a cave in which there is a pool. Two dragons live in that pool. By night, they fight so that the ground is shaken, and the building work is destroyed. By day they sleep. Expose the pool by day, and your men will come to no harm.'

Despite the protestations of the advisers, Vortigern gave orders for the ground beneath the foundations to be excavated. All of a sudden, a cry came from the men digging. The ground beneath them was falling inwards. There was a cave underneath them.

The hole into the cave was made bigger, so that men could go down with lights to see what lay within it. There was a pool, just as Merlin had said, and the water was stirring, as if a great creature breathed below its surface. The news was relayed to Vortigern, who looked slowly and meaningfully at his advisers, before giving orders for the pool to be drained.

The work was slow and hard, but at last, in the cold, dark cave, in the flickering light of the torches, two sleeping dragons were exposed to view; one red and the other white. Once again, messengers were sent to tell Vortigern what had been found. Merlin, still with the chains binding his slim wrists, stood before the King, and looked at him steadily.

'Will you go down and look at this sight?' he asked. Vortigern shivered and looked away.

'I will not!'

'Then order your men to leave the cave, for the sun is setting, and the dragons will awaken soon.'

Even as he spoke, the men in the cave saw the waters heave and boil, and the dragons appeared, breathing fire and smoke. Their fighting began before the men had escaped, and they turned to watch the battle. All night the dragons fought, sometimes the red gaining the advantage, at other times the white overcoming the other. Just before the sun began to rise, the red dragon was in the ascendant, but the white, driven to the edge of the pool, gathered its strength, and was about to rally, when the first rays of sunlight came over the mountain. The only knowledge that the men watching had of the coming of the dawn in that torch-lit cavern was that the dragons turned away from each other, and sank back into the water.

Vortigern turned to his advisers when the men returned to tell of what they had seen in the dark hollow beneath the mountain.

'What does this mean, these fighting dragons? What does it portend for us?'

Merlin laughed again. 'You ask these ignorant old men, these bewhiskered liars what is the meaning of the sights below the mountain? They know nothing. They can tell you nothing but lies and half-remembered verses of which they understand nothing. Send them away, O King. They cannot help you.'

'Tell us, then, arrogant boy! Tell us what these things mean,' thundered Vortigern.

'First I must ask you this,' said Merlin; 'Are you prepared to go down yourself into the cavern?'

'Why should I do that?' Vortigern demanded.

'The Cauldron of Ceridwen is found in many places. For you, O King, it lies beneath the mountain. For you it contains dragons. For other men, the challenge is different. But if you can tame the dragons in the pool, if you can cause the red and the white to be in peace waking, as they are in sleeping, then you are the true king of the Britons. If you cannot, there is another, yet unborn, who can, and his father shall be your death.'

Vortigern thought of going down into the darkness, to the dragon pool that this youth had called the Cauldron of Ceridwen. Tame the dragons? Cause them to be at peace waking as they are sleeping? What did it all mean? It was impossible! He turned to the old men shuffling and fearful in the corner.

'What has the goddess and her cauldron to do with me?' he shouted. One of them stepped forward.

'Sire, the red dragon is our own, and the white is the dragon of the Saxons. The red dragon will prevail! This is the meaning of the tarn in the cavern.'

Merlin laughed harshly.

'Believe that if you like, old man, but this is no scuffle between totems. Either the King takes up the challenge, or he does not. If he does not, look to yourselves. Will you end your days starving by the roadside?'

The advisers were, as the boy had said, no use to the king at all. They were now looking at each other, pale and frightened, whispering together. Vortigern drew his dagger from his belt and turned in a cold fury to Merlin, just as a messenger entered.

'Uther Pendragon is coming from Brittany!' the messenger cried; 'There is a great army at his heels! Prepare yourself, O King! It is said that he seeks you above all men, and will not rest until you are dead!'

'What!' shouted Vortigern; 'Uther Pendragon is on the sea?'

'No, Sire! He is landed with a great army of Breton men, and it is you that he seeks.'

Vortigern turned again to Merlin, but he was gone. The chains that bound him lay on the floor, but the boy himself had vanished. No-one had seen him go.

Vortigern fled from place to place, until at last he was besieged by Uther's army in a wooden fort on a Welsh hillside. Uther's men came with flaming torches, and Vortigern was consumed in the flaming ruins of his last redoubt.

✝

Many people visit Rosslyn, with many different purposes. Once a party of psychics came, and one of them, on the basis of sudden and direct experience, described William Sinclair, the founder of the chapel, as a true Merlin. Indeed, the Victorian painter Joseph Michael Gandy painted a picture entitled the Tomb of Merlin in 1815, and Rosslyn, William's tomb, was clearly the inspiration for it. The twin dragons on the west wall are a sign that William Sinclair, the initiate, the illuminatus, *had successfully met Ceridwen's challenge. The dragons are awake and in harmonious embrace.*

The twin dragons.

15. The Legend of the Holy Grail

We know that in the East, there exist paths of inner transformation, such as yoga, Zen Buddhism and others. But is there a path of spiritual enlightenment that is native to the western world? The short answer to that is: yes, there is, and the Holy Grail lies at the heart of it. However, the Grail is one of the most misunderstood themes in western culture. Part of the reason for this is that there are different versions of the medieval Grail stories in existence.

Our task here is not to describe any spiritual path, but simply to recall some of the versions of the Grail that are to be found in the literature of the past and present.

The jewelled chalice

The Holy Grail is often pictured as a rich chalice, and we are told that Joseph of Arimathea gave it to Jesus Christ; that He used it at the Last Supper, where He shared bread and wine with his closest disciples. We are then told that Joseph of Arimathea used this same chalice to gather up the blood of Christ that flowed from His wounds on the Cross of Golgotha.

There is an old legend that tells us that Joseph was thrown into prison for many years, suspected of a plot to remove the body of Jesus from the tomb, and so cheat the authorities. But Joseph took the chalice with him into his narrow prison cell, and was sustained by it, never aging, all the long years of his captivity.

The legend continues: Vespasian, Emperor of Rome heard of Christ's Passion from a knight who had been travelling in the Holy Land. Vespasian was fascinated by the stories that he heard of the humble teacher of love, who had been executed, but had risen from the dead. He travelled to Jerusalem, and tried to force the authorities in Jerusalem to produce the body of Christ. This they could not do, but one of the priests questioned told of the cell where Joseph was imprisoned. He was discovered showing no signs of age, and no sign of suffering. Through the orders of the Emperor, Joseph was set free. He and his sister and her husband, and a small group of pilgrims, left the Holy Land, and travelled to Europe.

Here, Joseph began a pilgrimage of his own, stopping in certain places to allow a few drops of the Holy Blood to fall on the earth. Such places became the object of pilgrimage themselves. The legend tells us that Joseph came at last to the south west of England, and could go no further. He wanted to travel as far as Ireland, but he died at Glastonbury.

The chalice that he bore was later sought by Knights of Arthur's Round Table, once Arthur and the knights had brought order into a moral chaos, through the code of chivalry which they upheld. The Grail appeared to Arthur at the Feast of Pentecost, and it was made clear that the Quest for the Grail was the new task of the Round Table; the culmination of their work in the world. The knights of Arthur who attained to the Fellowship of the Grail were Bors, Perceval and Galahad. Lancelot was vouchsafed a glimpse of the holy vessel, but because of the sinful love he had for Queen Guinevere, he could not be part of the company that celebrated Mass. He could do no more than to look on, while three Frenchmen, three Danes, three Irishmen and three Scotsmen, all of them knights, celebrated Mass with the Holy Grail itself at the centre of the ceremony.

The stone from the crown of Lucifer

The Red Knight Parzival was told by his uncle, the holy hermit Trevrezent, a somewhat different story, according to the tale told by Chrétien de

Troyes and Wolfram von Eschenbach; though it echoes in some respects the first account.

Trevrezent related that long before the creation of this world, there was a war in Heaven. Lucifer, the bright archangel, was cast out from among the Heavenly Host, and as he fell, a green stone was loosened from his crown. Sixty thousand angels had bestowed this crown upon him, and the stone was placed there by the Most High God. But now it fell to earth, where it was carved by angelic hands into a vessel of great beauty and exceeding worth.

After many ages had passed, the legend tells that it came into the hands of Joseph of Arimathea, who offered it to Jesus of Nazareth. He used it at the Last Supper, where He invited His disciples to eat and drink with Him, saying that the wine was His blood and the bread His body. The following day, Joseph used the same cup to hold some of the blood that flowed from the Cross.

He took this with him on his travels, and, as we have already learned, at certain places, poured a few drops of the Holy Blood on to the ground. But the most secret of the places visited by Joseph of Arimathea was the Hill of Montsalvasch.

The story now goes on to tell of a man named Titurisone. He was a virtuous man, and sorrow filled him, as he had no heir to continue his race. Following the advice of a wise soothsayer, he made a pilgrimage to the Holy Sepulchre, and there laid a golden crucifix upon the altar.

On his return, great was his joy to discover that his wife had borne him a son. This child was called Titurel, who grew to become a great warrior for the Christian faith.

One day, while Titurel was walking in solemn meditation in the woods, he was met by an angel, who told him in a voice of music that he had been chosen as the Guardian of the Holy Grail. He would find this precious thing on Montsalvasch, but he was to guard his tongue against letting the slightest mention of this task escape him, for the Grail was so precious a thing that none but the purest of heart could catch sight of even a glimpse of it.

Titurel sold all his worldly goods, except his sword and armour, with which he travelled to Montsalvasch, to protect it from all who would desecrate its sanctified ground. Yet he knew no more than this how to go forward in his destined path.

At last, he returned to the place where the angel had appeared to him, to try to discover what he should do next. As he stood gazing into the blue sky, he saw a cloud that appeared to beckon him onwards. He followed the cloud through trackless woods and desert ways until he came to a steep and perilous mountain. The ascent was difficult and dangerous, but at last he reached the summit, where he saw the Holy Grail, the brightly shining emerald vessel, held in invisible hands. He fell to his knees in wonder, giving thanks for this vision, all unaware of cries of welcome that came from the throats of men in armour, who called him their king. Once he became aware that there were others present, he asked them who they were. He learned that they called themselves Templars.

For many years Titurel and the Templars guarded the mountain from any who would attempt the climb with less than a pure heart. At last, he knew that he should build a temple to house the Grail. He and the knights set to work to clear the mountain top, and the summit was revealed as a smooth onyx of great size. Upon this foundation they set about building the shrine of the Holy Grail.

Now this temple was a hundred fathoms in diameter, and surrounding it were seventy two chapels, octagonal in shape. A tower six storeys high crowned each chapel, with a winding stair on the outside. At the centre was a tower twice as high as the others, resting on arches. The ceiling vaults were of sapphires and in the centre a plate of emerald, showing the Lamb of God represented in enamel. The altar stones were sapphires, symbolizing the propitiation of sins. Inside the cupola were shown the sun and moon, all made of diamond and topaz. The floor was all of clear crystal, with fish carved of onyx beneath, so that to stand on it was as if to stand on the sea itself. The windows were made of translucent stones, such as crystal and beryl; the towers were of precious stones, with gold inlaid, and their roofs were made of gold and blue enamel. Every tower was crowned with a cross of pure crystal, and an eagle with outspread wings atop each one. The summit of the main tower was capped with an immense carbuncle stone, to act as a guiding light to the Templars at night. And at the heart of the building, under the central dome, was a representation in miniature of the temple, and in this was placed the Holy Grail itself, but not by any human hand. Its invisible, angelic bearers placed it there. Upon the vessel, from time to time, there appeared a message from the Heavenly Heights, which the guardians of the Grail would read in the deepest awe and reverence.

It was the holy vessel that sustained the men whose duty was to guard it, and gave them long life, granting them all that they needed to live.

The cup of jasper

There is, however, yet a third version, and this tale we owe again to the modern seership of Judith von Halle. According to her account, Joseph of Arimathea took the cup that was used at the Last Supper. It was neither a rich chalice, according to this account, nor was it a green stone: it was made of jasper. He did, as the legends tell, scoop up as much of the precious blood as he could from the depression at the foot of the Cross where it gathered, and travel with the Holy Blood through the Mediterranean world, coming to the South of France. He did not travel alone, but Mary Magdalene accompanied him, and preached beside him. She could not speak on her own account, as women in those days were not given respectful listening. Instead, she spoke of what her brother John the Evangelist had witnessed, for much of this she, too, had witnessed with her own eyes, and could speak of with authority.

It was Joseph's practice, as indeed the foregoing legends tell, to pour a few drops of Christ's blood on to the earth in certain places.

One such place was a rock, and around this rock was built a castle. Though not as rich in its materials as the Grail Castle of the legend, it was nevertheless built with great cunning. The long chamber where those who ordained the construction of the building welcomed guests and dined was carefully made to deceive the eye. It was, in fact, shorter than it looked. Beyond the farther wall was a hidden chamber, and in the centre of that chamber was the rock upon which Joseph let fall some drops of the Holy Blood. Within this chamber, the very highest initiation of the Templar Knights took place, for it was Templars who built this castle. Only the twelve Grand Masters of the Order celebrated the ceremony of initiation, under the guidance of the one Grand Master of them all.

The Templars had as their highest ideal to become vessels of the Christ. They believed that the secret of this was to transform the very blood in their veins through their earthly and spiritual striving, so that their blood became, literally, Christ's blood.

This was what they understood by the Holy Grail: transformation of their own being through a lifetime of work dedicated to Christ.

†

There are clear signs in Rosslyn Chapel that those who ordered the building held the memory of the Templars in deep veneration. Earl William Sinclair, Gilbert de la Haye and Earl William's first wife, Elizabeth Douglas, were trying to build a Chapel of the Grail. It is also clear from a deep reading of the carvings in Rosslyn that the chapel was a place of initiation, and a part of the Grail tradition.

16. Saint Margaret

The next three stories come from historical accounts, rather than old legends, or tales of saints and wonders.

The south aisle in Rosslyn is notable for its feminine qualities. Here we see Margaret holding a fragment of the True Cross, and William 'the Seemly' Sinclair together in a carving in the westernmost window. Margaret's hair is shown following almost a crescent pattern, with braids curling upwards, as a sign of her deep spirituality. The only other figures in the chapel to have this feature are angels. Margaret was certainly a human being, rather than an angel, but after miracles were reported as happening in connection with her remains, she was canonized in 1250. Her saint's day is June 10. Margaret was of great importance to the Sinclair family, and she remains one of their patron saints, and as such, of course, is remembered in the structure of the chapel.

Ever since the ninth century, and the days of King Alfred of Wessex, England had been threatened by invasion from Denmark. Indeed, the eastern part of the island had come under Danish rule. Two hundred years later, affairs between England and Denmark were still such that the English King Edward the Atheling, fearing for his young family, had his daughter Margaret taken to Hungary, where she could be brought up in safety, and given an education worthy of a royal princess.

Saint Margaret, bearing a fragment of the True Cross, with William 'the Seemly' Sinclair.

Whatever she learned in Hungary, Margaret certainly developed a habit of piety that ran deep in her soul, and was a well-established part of her character by the time it was deemed safe to bring her back to England, in the reign of King Edward the Confessor.

But now a new peril loomed. The Duke of Normandy, William, led an invading army to England, landing at Pevensey Bay, near Hastings, and quickly and efficiently overran the country.

Margaret was forced to flee with some trusted knights, including some from her Hungarian household, and they sailed northwards. Even the elements were against them. Their ship was blown off course, and they were forced to make landfall in Fife.

The news reached the Scottish king Malcolm Canmore that an English princess had arrived in Scotland, and was in some distress, having to flee her native country and now shipwrecked in his country. Malcolm knew about flight, as he himself had fled from Macbeth, the killer of his father, Duncan. He had taken refuge in England for some time, and then returned to defeat Macbeth, and slay him. (Shakespeare, it is true, tells the story rather differently.)

Malcolm sent one of his most trusted knights, Sir William, 'the Seemly' Sinclair, to escort the princess to his royal household at Edinburgh. Margaret was known for her beauty as much as for her piety, and when Malcolm saw her, escorted by William Sinclair and the faithful Hungarian knight Ladislaus Lecelin, he was determined to make her his wife.

Margaret had no wish to marry, and wished instead to devote her life to the study and deepening of her religion. She wished to live as chastely as a nun, but Malcolm was an insistent and patient suitor, and in the year 1070, Margaret agreed to become his wife. She was twenty-five years old.

In Scotland at the time there was a rich and long-abiding stream of Christianity through which the Celtic spirituality expressed itself. The priests of this Celtic Christianity were called the *Celi-Dé*, the servants of God. Margaret admired these people greatly, and was at pains to rescue them from the zeal of those who wished to impose a single rule of worship in the land. In fact, Margaret was in favour of uniting worship in Scotland, so that all of the people could, wherever they were, find a form of service with which they were familiar, and which would unite them with other worshippers in England and abroad. Perhaps her greatest wish was to heal the bloody rifts between England and Scotland through unity in worship. She invited English priests to help this process, but always did what she could to protect the *Celi-Dé* from attack, or accusations of heresy, or poor treatment of any kind. The watchword of her faith was tolerance and loving acceptance rather than rigid adherence to dogma.

Having experienced herself at first hand the wildness of the weather around Scottish shores, she instituted the Queen's Ferry, across the Forth, to help pilgrims on their way to Saint Andrews, to worship at the shrine of the saint, so that they did not have to brave the open sea, or the long and rough way over land. North Queensferry and South Queensferry remain today, in the shadow of the great Forth Bridges, as a testament to Queen Margaret's generosity to pilgrims.

All the indications are that Margaret was a loving wife to Malcolm, presenting him with eight children, three of whom became kings later. Still, she found time to found hostels for travellers, to extend regular and generous charity to the poor, to feed orphans, taking the youngest on her lap to do so. Similarly, it was her regular practice to wash the feet of the poor. Apart from her regular self-imposed duties of charity, she founded hospitals, monasteries and churches, while her more secular work included bringing a taste of European manners, customs and ceremony to the Scottish court. Her influence was much appreciated in this sphere, and the Scottish court gained a wide reputation for its culture under her aegis.

One of the places that Margaret made sure was brought into a state of good repair was the monastery at Iona. This was the island from where Saint Columba had started his ministry, and it had long been the burial place of the kings of Scotland. Margaret was sensitive to its importance in the Scottish psyche.

Perhaps it was a feeling of duty to Margaret that inspired Malcolm to lead five, possibly more, invasions into England. The only English prince to survive the Norman invasion was Edgar the Atheling, Margaret's brother, and it is clear that Malcolm was keen to see Edgar on the throne of England.

During the last of these invasions, Malcolm and his eldest son were ambushed and killed at Alnwick in Northumberland. Margaret had been undergoing a series of punishing fasts at this time, and lay sick in bed when her second son Edmund came to bring her the news. It was too great a blow for her to survive.

As she lay on her deathbed, she held tightly in her hands something that she had brought with her from Hungary: a fragment of the True Cross, itself formed into a crucifix. She had founded Dunfermline Abbey with the view to building a house for this sacred relic, and now felt the need of whatever comfort it could afford her in her last hours.

Three days after the death of Malcolm, Margaret died, in the year 1093. She was forty-seven years old.

Three of her sons followed Malcolm on to the throne of Scotland: Edgar, Alexander and David. It was this same David who greeted Hugh de Payens and the first Templars when they arrived in Scotland. This marked the beginning of a long and important relationship between the Knights Templar and Scotland; a relationship honoured in Rosslyn Chapel.

17. The Rise and Fall of the Templars

Dr Tim Wallace-Murphy says in The Templar Legacy and the Masonic Inheritance in Rosslyn Chapel *that there are five signs by which we can recognize a Templar church: a dove in flight with an olive branch in its beak; a five-pointed star; a floriated cross; the Agnus Dei, or Lamb of God, and finally the Veil of Veronica, showing the face of Christ. These are all present in Rosslyn, and a strong, obstinate tradition links the chapel with the Templars. To the left of the North Door, inside the chapel, is a carving showing the Crucifixion.*

Some maintain that the Crucifixion scene is a double reference: the Crucifixion of Jesus Christ on Golgotha, and at the same time, a representation of the execution of Jacques de Molay, the last Grand Master of the Templar Knights. What links it to the central event of the Christian calendar are the carvings close at hand of other scenes connected with the Crucifixion; the women sorrowing, shown on the capital of a pillar opposite, and a carving showing the stone rolled away from the mouth of the tomb. But in the Crucifixion scene, the cross is alone, the two thieves are missing; the cross is not elevated above the people, but the victim's feet are as close to the ground as the others; the cross itself is T-shaped, rather than the shape familiar to us from so many other representations. This last could, of course, be a result of wilful damage. However, it seems a strange place for such an important event to be placed: up beside the corner of the North Door.

*A little farther along, in the corner between an architrave and the north wall is a carving in relief of a man with a dog on a leash. This is said to represent the Pope, Clement V as a blind man, being led by Philippe le Bel, the King of France, whose rage against the Templars brought about the destruction of the Order.**

Another notable carving in the northern side of the chapel is in the lower right hand corner of a window, where we see the figure of a bearded man holding an open book, and pointing to a particular page. The book is the Bible, or at least the Gospel of John, and the page indicated is the seventeenth chapter; the so-called High Priestly Prayer. This chapter was an important part of Templar initiation practice.

Who were the Templars, these men, who were on the one hand so revered, and on the other so reviled and hated?

The origins of the Templars

In the year 1118, nine knights arrived in Jerusalem from France. Chief among them were Hugh de Payens and Godfrey of Omer. They made their way to the palace of the King of Jerusalem, for in those days, the Holy Land was governed by European Crusader forces. These nine men were already united in a spiritual sect dedicated to the Holy Grail. It was their wish to found a new order, both monastic and military. They would live like monks but train as soldiers, and their first avowed task would be to guard the pilgrim routes to the Holy Land. They became known as the Poor Knights of Christ and of the Temple of Solomon. For nine years they remained in Jerusalem, living in comparative poverty. Hugh de Payens and Godfrey of Omer had only one warhorse between them, which they shared. This became symbolic of their ideals, and was acknowledged in their seal, which shows two men on one horse, signifying the vow of poverty, and the sharing among them of what worldly goods they had.

---

* The dog is also a common hidden meaning of the Dominican Inquisition, said to be a play on words in the Latin Dominicani (the Dominicans) = *Domini canes* (the Dogs of God)

The Crucifixion — or the execution of Jacques de Molay?

The High Priest's Prayer, Gospel of John, Chapter 17.

During those first nine years, they sought permission to excavate under the site of the Temple of Solomon, from where they took away two trunk loads of things, but no-one knows exactly what. Some believe these things to have been placed deep in the crypt beneath Rosslyn, but no clear proof of this has ever been found.

From these fairly humble and industrious beginnings, the Knights of the Temple, or Templars, were brought in under the protection of the Church, through the agency of Bernard de Clairvaux, a Cistercian abbot, who understood and championed their ideals. Pope Honorius confirmed the Order, and decreed that they should wear a white tunic, to which Pope Eugenius III later added the red cross over the breast. They took as their patroness Mary the Mother of Christ, and they held the Archangel Michael in special reverence. Beneath their armour and mail, next to the skin, they wore a red cord, symbolizing that they strove to overcome the demands of the organs of appetite that lay below the cord. It was also a constant reminder that every drop of their blood belonged to Christ. Here we see their relationship to the Holy Grail. The Templar ideal was to strive to change through their prayer and inner resolve, the very blood in their veins, so that it became Christ's blood. To strengthen this resolve, they took vows of poverty and chastity and strove in their initiation practices to put aside their own wishes and ambitions and try to realize the Christ within themselves. They, too, were Sons of the Widow; men who acknowledged the widowed Soul of the World, and did all they could to welcome the Bridegroom into the world.

As soon as they had been recognized by the Church, Hugh de Payens and his company rode across Europe, seeking interviews with kings and noblemen, to draw support to their cause. In Scotland they found their strongest, most enthusiastic support. King David I, youngest son of Malcolm Canmore and Queen Margaret, received them with all honours, and made the Templars 'guardians over his morals by day and by night'. The first secular building that was erected by the Templars in Europe was the Commandery at Balantrodoch, a little village some eight miles from Edinburgh, and near to Roslin. The village was so associated with the Templar order that its name changed to Temple, though hardly a stone of the original Templar buildings remains visible today, apart from the corner of an outlying wall.

The Agnus Dei.

Pope Clement V as blind man led by the dog, King Philippe IV of France.

The growth of the Templar Order

The Templars became known for their fighting skill and their extraordinary bravery. They would not surrender in a fight or retreat, even if outnumbered three to one. Notwithstanding all their martial skill however, they were unequal to the task of overcoming the Saracen forces under Saladin. Those who were captured met their execution silently and without complaint, though at the Battle of Acre, they fought, famously, to the last man, without surrender.

Once forced out of the Holy Land, they set up headquarters in Paris, and on Cyprus. They still received the support of rich and powerful men, who gave them lands and property. With the knowledge and skills that they had learned in the Middle East, they brought in methods of architecture which they put to use in building churches, bridges and roads, and in the founding of towns. They introduced a system of bank credit very similar to the credit card of today. It was also the Templars who discovered the art of twice cooking a small wheaten cake; they invented the biscuit. But it was the construction of churches for which they were remembered. For them, to build a church was symbolic of the inner task of building a spiritual temple. The transformation of bricks and mortar into something dedicated to the spirit was an outer sign of the transformation of the substance of the earth into a place fit for the New Jerusalem, and of the transformation of the flesh and blood of their bodies into a fit vessel for the Christ.

They became known, respected and often feared and hated all across Europe and beyond, as they spread their influence over the course of two centuries. But they made a powerful and unforgiving enemy. Philippe IV of France was known as Philippe 'the Fair'. Handsome though his outsides may have looked, in his dealings with the Templars he showed vicious and treacherous cruelty.

The enmity of Philippe le Bel

His wars against the English had bled his country almost dry. One day in the year 1306, while riding through Paris in his coach, he was recognized by the mob, which pursued him, and would have torn him to pieces. He leaped from his carriage and ran to the nearest house, and banged on the door in fear of his life. This building, it turned out, was the headquarters of the Temple Knights. They took him in, and two of them went out to calm the crowd. Philippe saw how they listened to these men, and dispersed on their orders, and was filled with envy and chagrin as much as relief that his life had been saved. These men had a mastery that he lacked. He pressed them to show him round their house, and here he saw how much wealth these men held in trust. This could pay his debts, but he was wary of them, and the power that they could wield. He knew that the English King Henry had been told by Templars: 'You shall be king as long as you are just.'

These impressions worked on Philippe, and mingled in his breast with another emotion. As a young man, he had applied to become a Templar knight himself, but had been rejected by the Order. This rejection still rankled. A criticism that some made of the Templars was that they recruited among their ranks some men that were not worthy of the name of Templar. Philippe was not one of those. He had been refused, and he still felt angry. The thought began to take shape in his soul: to get revenge on the Templars; to gain their wealth and to destroy their Order.

The seat of the Popes at this time was not Rome but Avignon. Philippe had already made sure that a favourite of his, one Bertrand de Got, should be made Pope, on five conditions. The first four he named at once, but he waited to name the fifth. Bertrand de Got was inaugurated as Pope, with the name Clement V. The fifth condition was now named: help Philippe to destroy the Order of the Poor Knights of the Temple.

Philippe went to work with patience and subtlety. There were many who had fallen foul of the Templars, and many who resented the extent of their power and influence. Here already were allies for Philippe. There was also, here and there, a waif word about strange rituals conducted by the Templars; hints, even of heretical practices. With his intelligence sources now as widespread as the Church, through the agency of Clement, two renegade Templars were found; men who had been thrown out of the Order. These were Roffi Dei, from Florence, and the Prior of Montfaucon, who had been sentenced to life imprisonment by the Grand Master of the Templars for his many crimes. They were more than ready to work against the Order.

Templar knights were arrested in various places, and put to torture. There were certain members of the Dominican Order who found themselves only too willing to use torture to extract confessions from such powerful and virtuous men.

The arrest of Jacques de Molay

The great prize was still to be achieved. The Grand Master himself, Jacques de Molay, was in Cyprus when he received an invitation to confer with the Pope on the subject of the Holy Land, and how it was to be won back from the Musulman armies.

De Molay arrived in France in 1307. Before travelling to Paris however, he stopped at a castle in the South West of France of which today, nothing but ruins remain. Here, he gathered the twelve Masters of the Order. The castle where they met was built in such a way that the long chamber was actually shorter than it appeared to the eye, and hidden chambers could exist, whose existence visitors would not suspect. Here in these hidden chambers, the very highest of the Templar initiations could take place, but only after a series of other, lesser initiations had already been carried out elsewhere.

The Grand Master de Molay had received an inkling of what awaited the Templars. He advised the other Masters that they should perform their highest initiation again, but this time, in reverse, in order to give it back to those lofty spiritual sources whence it sprang. Many of the Masters were not happy that the Order should cut itself off from the highest sources of its inspiration, but for de Molay, it was necessary. If the Order was to perish, then it should do so in full awareness of its original mission. *Non nobis, Domine, non nobis, sed Nomini Tuo da gloriam!* (Not unto us, O Lord, not unto us, but unto Thy name be the glory given). Self-sacrifice in Christ's name was demanded of each man.

After the visit to the castle in the south, Jacques de Molay made his way north with sixty knights to Paris, with 150,000 golden florins and twelve horses laden with silver. These funds were deposited in the Temple in the city. Philippe then greeted him, treating him with every courtesy and respect. He made de Molay godfather of one of his sons, and invited him to be a pall-bearer at the funeral of his sister-in-law the following day. Even as he made the Grand Master welcome, sealed orders were being sent out to order the arrest of all Templars in France.

These arrests took place on Friday, October 13, 1307, including that of the Grand Master. He was imprisoned for several years and, under torture, confessed to all the crimes of which the Templars were accused: heresy; sodomy; spitting on the cross; worshipping a demonic head; worshipping an idol made of the flayed skin of a man, stuffed with straw and basted with the fat of roasted children; worshipping the devil in the form of a cat; burning the bodies of dead Templars and giving the ashes to younger members of the Order to eat and drink, mixed in with their food: accusations that tell us more about their accusers than the men accused.

At last the Grand Master was led out with Guy, the Grand Preceptor, to be slow-roasted over a charcoal fire on March 18, 1313. At his execution, Jacques de Molay took back all of which he had been accused — except one detail, the spitting on the cross — saying that he had confessed under the hardest duress. He also warned Philippe and Clement that they would each stand before the Judgment Seat of God within the year. Philippe and Clement did, indeed, die, within the year.

The destruction of the Order

Thus the Order came to an end. Philippe and the English King Edward II divided up the spoils between them. Clement V complained at first that he was being left out of the division of spoils, and published a Bull in exculpation of the Templars: the so-called Document of Chinon. However, the two kings relented, and allowed him a share of the loot, and Clement threw in his lot once again with his royal masters. He still complained, later, that he had been cheated.

In other countries, responses differed. In Italy, much of the land and property belonging to the Templars was given to the Order of the Knights Hospitallers, though they were heavily taxed on them, so that they almost had to disband themselves. A Papal Bull dated May 6, 1312, suppressed the Order of the Temple, but in Spain and Cyprus, the Order was acquitted of all guilt. In Germany, a Grand Master led a band of Templar Knights into a meeting of bishops, fully armed and armoured, and angrily rebutted all accusations against the Order. He received no argument from the Holy Fathers. In Portugal, the king simply ordered the Templars to change their name to the Knights of Christ, and they continued business much as before. We shall see in the next chapter what happened in Scotland.

Yet the Templars still continued to influence life in Europe. In Portugal, Christopher Columbus was closely connected through his family to the Knights of Christ. Templar fleets, with the skull and crossbones flag, had sailed across the Atlantic in search of plants and medicines, but had kept secret their knowledge of the land that they called Lamerika.

But the days of the Templar Order had come to an end. Some members joined other military monastic orders, such as the Knights Hospitallers, or the Teutonic Knights. The Order that protected pilgrims, invented banking systems, built towns, cities, roads, bridges and churches was finished. In fact, Jacques de Molay and the twelve Masters had themselves abolished the Order in a way that Philippe could never have understood, before he carried out his revenge. The carvings in Rosslyn are a homage to those men; a way of preserving a memory of their greatness.

18. The Heart of Robert the Bruce

Almost hidden in the east end of the chapel, in the Lady Chapel is a face with staring eyes, the brows gathered as though in concentration, while the surrounding stonework seems about to swallow it, like a swamp. The face is clean-shaven, and a close inspection shows damage, as though of battle scars and leprosy. This face is the death mask of King Robert the Bruce.

The body of Robert the Bruce lies buried in Dunfermline, and his heart has recently been discovered in Melrose Abbey. It is no surprise that the great fourteenth century king of Scotland is honoured in Rosslyn.

Bruce's struggle for the Crown of Scotland

Robert the Bruce was born in 1274 into a noble family, with royal connections on his father's side. His mother belonged to the Gaels of the West of Scotland; a fact which was to have some helpful influence for him later.

With the tragic, accidental death of King Alexander III, the throne of Scotland became the centre of controversy. At first, Alexander's only remaining relative, his young grand-daughter, Margaret, the 'Maid of Norway' was the only contender for the throne from the House of Canmore.

At the age of eight, she sailed to Scotland from Norway, where she had been brought up. However, she died, apparently of the effects of the sea voyage. This left several contenders for the throne, among them Robert's grandfather, John Comyn, known as 'the Contender', and John Balliol. The English King Edward I was asked to arbitrate in the dispute, and he chose Balliol, a man whom he knew he could control. Indeed, he subjected him to various humiliations before forcing him to abdicate by invading Scotland.

The Bruce family refused to back Balliol. At first, they supported Edward's invasion of Scotland in 1296 that removed Balliol from the throne, but when William Wallace, the Braveheart of popular mythology, rose in rebellion against Edward I, Robert the Bruce supported the Scottish rebel. This rebellion was put down fiercely by Edward.

Bruce was allowed to keep his lands, in spite of having supported the Braveheart Wallace, and he became one of the so-called Guardians of Scotland. Another of these was John Comyn. There was no love lost between Comyn and Bruce.

Comyn murderously attacked Bruce in Selkirk Forest, in the year 1299, the matter between them being the Crown of Scotland. Comyn claimed descent from a by-blow of Donal Bane, son of King Duncan I, whereas Bruce claimed direct and legitimate descent from King David I, who was the youngest son of Saint Margaret, Queen of Scotland, and was known to have made the Templars 'guardians over his soul by day and by night'.

In 1306, the Bruce took his dagger and stabbed John Comyn on the chancel steps of Greyfriars Church in Dumfries. Comyn's uncle tried to go to his aid, but he was struck down in his turn by Christopher Seton, Bruce's brother-in-law. Monks came forward to nurse the wounded man, but when asked if Comyn was indeed dead, Bruce exclaimed that he would 'mak siccar' and went back to finish the job, dragging the dying Comyn back to the steps before the altar to do so.

Bruce was excommunicated for this violent act which polluted a sanctified building, and all of Scotland was placed under an interdict. This meant that mass was not celebrated, baptisms could not take place, funerals and weddings were hugger-mugger affairs at the church gate, if anywhere. It was a spiritual disaster for the country.

But something had changed, or come into its own in the soul of Robert the Bruce. He now felt his destiny as certainly as the weapons he took in his hands. Edward I proclaimed the Bruce outlaw, but his response was to ride through the country seeking support for his claim to the throne. He had himself crowned at Scone in 1306, by two Archbishops, Lamberton of Saint Andrews and Wishart of Glasgow.

The outlaw king was deposed soon after this by the English King Edward II; his family imprisoned, and three of his brothers executed. Bruce fled to an island off the coast of Antrim in Northern Ireland, a short trip across the sea, but soon returned to Scotland to gain support for his reinstatement as king, and to wage a guerrilla war against the English. The story is told that, in his brief exile, he had entered a cave, and, while watching a spider patiently spinning its web in spite of all obstacles in its path, saw this as a sign to himself to continue his path to the throne of Scotland; a Scotland separate and independent of England. The picture of entering a cave is often connected with communion with one's higher self. Violent and forceful man as he was, there was that in Bruce that saw not only his destiny clearly, but that of his country, and the spiritual ground upon which that country stood.

The death mask of Robert the Bruce.

The arrival of the Templars

During these events, the Templars were the victims of the French King's treachery and deceit, outlined in an earlier chapter. However, not all of the members of the Order in France were arrested. Some escaped with the Templar fleet, which had been moored at La Rochelle, in Brittany. They sailed northwards, between Britain and Ireland, keeping close to the Irish coast. There were not many commanderies in Ireland, but those that existed were stripped of their arms by the escaping Templars, who made their way finally to Argyll, where they settled. Many of their graves are still to be found scattered in the West of Scotland.

Argyll at the time had recently been freed from Viking domination following the Battle of Largs in 1263, but the undisputed ruler of the region was Macdonald, Lord of the Isles. The escaping Templars were safe under the protection of Macdonald, and Argyll was very difficult to reach, except by sea, at that time. The islands and Argyll however, came under the spiritual guidance of the Archbishop of Trondheim, who never visited his distant flock. It is unlikely that the influence of the bishop was either felt or feared, very much.

The Holyrood trial

Templars in Edinburgh were already feeling the tension of the destructive forces ranged against them by the French and British kings. Edward II and Philippe IV were dividing the loot that their campaign against the Templars had yielded, and now, in 1309, a papal envoy, one John Soleirio, arrived in Edinburgh to oversee the trial of two members of the Order, held at Holyrood.

There were plenty of witnesses to testify against the knights, including two members of the Sinclair family. However, what was most noticeable about the charges against them was that they were mild, compared with what had been adduced in more severe courts in France, Italy and England. They were accused, for instance, of being bullying neighbours, and of having secret rituals, though these were not specified. Neither was any evidence brought forward that had been achieved through torture in other courts, notably that of the Inquisition. This indicates a marked difference in the style and mental atmosphere of this Scottish trial, as opposed to those farther away.

The president of the court was Archbishop Lamberton of Saint Andrews, who had supported Robert the Bruce to the extent of assisting at his coronation at Scone. As the trial progressed, the court was held in a state of suspense — possibly for the benefit of the papal envoy — over the approach, ever nearer, of the outlaw king. The day before the verdict was due to be brought in, Soleirio left to return to the continent, satisfied that justice was being done in Holyrood.

It is unlikely that he would have rejoiced at the verdict, however. In Scots law, there were three possible verdicts: Guilty, Not Guilty and Not Proven. The latter implied that though the guilt of the accused was morally accepted by the court, the evidence had been insufficient to secure a conviction. Thus the court at Holyrood had clearly done all in its power to uphold the wishes of the neighbouring kings, but reason, forensic logic and justice could bring in no other verdict. The two Templars were set free. The case against them had not been proved.

In time, however, the property of the Temple in Scotland was handed over to the Hospitallers in Edinburgh, who made it clear in their acceptance that they were holding the lands and goods in trust, until such time as they might be returned to their rightful owners.

Bannockburn

In 1314, Robert the Bruce, the King of Scotland, led an army against the forces of the English. Among the troops rallying to his cause came an army from Argyll. Bruce's Gaelic antecedents had helped him to persuade Macdonald, Lord of the Isles, to send troops in support. Macdonald was effectively a law unto himself, and felt under no obligation to Bruce, but the Scottish king's diplomatic approach, as one ruler to another, couched in good Gaelic, was enough persuasion for the Lord of the Isles. And among those troops from Argyll were a number of the newcomers, not fighting as Templars, but as vassals to Macdonald; though there is an old tradition that the Templar battle flag, the black and white *Beauséant* was flown at Bannockburn.

There is a long-held tradition in Scottish freemasonry — and the tale is still told to this day — that Bruce himself welcomed the fleeing Templars, remembering the great impression that this Order of chivalry made upon his ancestor David I. Bruce organized their reception into the Freemasons' Lodge at Kilwinning. Here we see a clear connection between Bruce and the Templars, and the Templar influence in Rosslyn is bound to honour this tradition of support from a king who was responsible for maintaining Scotland's independence from an oppressor such as Edward of England, who was quick to divide the spoils of the Templars when they were disestablished in England.

The Scots were triumphant at Bannockburn, and an independent Scottish monarchy was re-established thanks in no small measure to the arrival of the Argyll Templars, if we are to credit the Masonic tradition. However, supporter of the Templar cause though he was, it was too late for Bruce to do anything to help to restore the Knights of the Temple to their former power.

The Declaration of Arbroath and the Bruce's death

In 1316, Bruce's brother, another Edward, became High King of Ireland, but was killed in battle two years later. Edward II refused to accept Bruce's right to the Scottish throne, claiming the overlordship of Scotland as his. But in 1320, the Scottish Earls, Barons and 'community of the realm' wrote to Pope John XXII declaring that Robert the Bruce was their rightful monarch. This was the famous Declaration of Arbroath. Four years later, the Pope recognized Robert the Bruce as the King of an independent Scotland. The Treaty of Corbeil renewed the Auld Alliance between France and Scotland, which demanded that Scotland would support France if war broke out between France and England. The Scottish victory at Bannockburn was reinforced even more strongly in 1322, at the Battle of Bylands, in which Robert the Bruce and his armies, including those Templars who had settled in Argyll, pursued the retreating English as far as York, and Edward II himself came close to being captured. This yet more ignominious defeat was to weigh heavily against Edward a few years later, when, in 1327 the English deposed him in favour of his son, and the tensions between the countries slackened, except along the borders, where cattle raids and guerrilla attacks continued for many years.

Robert the Bruce died in 1329. At his death he asked that his heart be taken to Jerusalem to be buried there, since he had never been able to undertake the crusade that he had promised to do to expiate his sin of the murder of Comyn. A group of knights took the Bruce's heart, and set off, but got no further than Spain. Among the escort was a member of the Sinclair family. Here, while fighting in the vanguard of the army of King Alfonso XI of Castile and Leon, they were surrounded at the battle of Tebas de Ardales. It was the bearer of Bruce's heart, Sir James Douglas, who threw the casket containing the royal organ into the midst of the Moors, with the cry (according to a colourful legend): 'Brave heart that ever foremost led, forward as thou wast wont! And I shall follow thee, or else shall die!'

The little group of Scots knights was defeated, and only one lived to take the heart back to Scotland. This was Sir William Keith, who, having broken his arm before the battle, could not take part. He retrieved the heart in its silver casket from the field of battle, and brought it back to Scotland.

Robert the Bruce traced his descent from David I, the great champion and pupil of the Templars. Templar knights assisted, according to the legend, at the decisive Battle of Bannockburn, and Bruce, true to the ideals of the Order of the Poor Knights of Christ and the Temple of Solomon, felt that his heart belonged in Jerusalem. It was buried in fact, in Melrose, in the grounds of the Cistercian Abbey, which lies in a green and pleasant valley in the shadow of the Eildon Hills. The rest of Bruce's body is buried at the ancient seat of the Scottish kings, Dunfermline. It is, surely, fitting that a chapel built by the Sinclair family should honour the memory of the King who saved Scotland from becoming a province of England, and whose last wish was to have his heart laid beside those Templars who died fighting in the Holy Land.

In the death mask, Bruce's eyes are open, looking with fierce concentration southwards, towards the lands of his enemies. Meanwhile, his angel offers his heart to the Founder of the Law and the Keeper of the Covenant with God, Moses.

The heart of Robert the Bruce.

19. The Rose Cross: A Fantasy of Rosslyn

The road from Edinburgh to Fairmilehead was dark and cold. Two men rode, keeping close together, up the hill. Behind them the city lay. Looking back, the younger man could discern the shape of the castle. Lights burned in one or two of the few houses that lay between the city and the Pentland Hills.

'How much further?' asked the younger man.

'We meet your guide at Fairmilehead,' said the other.

'And you? Will you not come with us?'

'I will not. Ye'll hae company enough.'

At the crown of the hill, a man rode out from the cover of the trees and greeted the older man.

'Hail Brother.'

'Of the roses and of the gold.'

'And of the cross.'

They spoke together the next line of their greeting.

'And blessed be God who gave us this sign.'

The young man watched as the two others leaned forward and showed each other scrolls hung with seals, though anything written on them was unreadable in the darkness.

'This is the young brother?' asked the newcomer.

'Aye. I gie him intae your hands, brother.' He turned to the younger man.

'Dismount,' he ordered curtly.

'Are we arrived? I thought — I mean, I had it in my mind that it was a longer journey we were taking.'

He dismounted as he spoke. The man who had accompanied him from the city dismounted too, but the newcomer remained mounted. His horse was a big black courser. The young man's guide led him to the mounted man.

'Up ye get,' he said, 'I'll gie ye a hand.'

He helped the young man to climb on to the big horse's back behind the rider, who turned towards him, holding something like a small sack.

'Here. Put this on.'

The young man hesitated, but took the sack, and pulled it over his head. The rider began to move off, but the guide was calling through the cold air.

'I'll take your horse tae Wilson's stable. Ye'll can get him again there.'

The young man waved, but was quick to put his arms round the rider again as they moved southwards over the rough roads.

The six miles that they rode seemed much longer to the young man deprived as he was of sight. At first he was afraid that the bag would be suffocating, but it let in sufficient air for him to breathe easily enough. Partly in preparation for what was to come, and partly from a kind of respect for the rider, he spoke not at all. The other said nothing on the journey either. The young man rehearsed in his mind the rituals that had led him to this strange ride through the darkness.

His name was Michael Edrom. He had been taken to a house in the bustling High Street of Edinburgh, near the top of the Castle Hill. The man who led him was an apothecary who had been recommended to him by a friend who belonged to the same brotherhood of which Michael was a member. But now Michael sought a deeper knowledge of the mysteries. He had managed to convince the warden of his lodge that he was worthy to be considered for a higher initiation.

'Aye, I kent your faither well,' the warden had said, 'he wis a guid sowel. A man o' craft, mind ye; no yin o' thae speculative chiels. Gin ye follow his example, ye'll no go faur wrang. I'll scrieve a letter tae the mannie that'll can help ye tae yer next step on the journey.'

He paused over his desk where paper, ink and quill pen sat ready.

'Thank you, sir,' said Michael. 'I'll do all I can not to disappoint you, I promise.'

'Hut tut tut,' the warden said. 'Na na, laddie. I can see ye're tae be trustit.'

Could he really, Michael wondered; and if so; how? Somehow he felt that the old man was not just showing good manners, but judgment of his character, and he felt a waif wisp of pride, which he managed to dispel before it could establish itself.

Grailed Cross in the north-east of Rosslyn chapel, the only one with a rose at the centre.

The smell of smoke in the street caught at his lungs at times, making him cough. People poured in and out of the high houses, into and out of the deep, narrow closes. Shouts and cried were all about him. The gutters ran with foul-smelling night waste. A troop of soldiers from the castle, with partisans or pikes over their shoulders, tramped down the cobbled street, pushing and elbowing the busy citizens from their path.

'In here,' said his companion suddenly. A sign hung over the street door, showing a pelican, pecking at its breast to feed its young. He was led up a winding stair to a room where three men sat at a table where lay lantern, lit, pen, ink and paper and two red cords. Nothing was said by way of introduction.

'You are Michael Edrom?' asked the oldest of the three, seated in the middle. Michael recognized the letter that the warden of his lodge had sent in his hands.

'I am,' he replied.

'And do you, Michael firmly intend to become a pupil of true wisdom?'

'I do.'

'Leave your sword here. Your hands will be bound with this cord, and this shall be put around your neck. Not here, but at the place of initiation.'

Michael was told more of what to expect, though he guessed that there were yet some surprises awaiting him.

That had been in the summer. Now it was early spring, and they were arriving at their journey's end. The young man could still see nothing, but had an impression of closeness to a building. The rider led him carefully to a doorway, where he stopped, and put a cord with a slip-knot over the young man's head, and tightened it, though not too tightly, at his throat. Michael's hands were tied. Then, the rider knocked at the door nine times. The door opened, and the doorkeeper asked: 'Who is there?'

'An earthly body holding the spiritual man imprisoned in ignorance.'

'What is to be done to him?'

'Kill his body and purify his spirit.'

'Then bring him to the place of justice.'

Michael was led into the building. He could sense candles burning in a large, cold space, and human figures around him. A light pressure on his shoulder forced him to kneel. Someone stood at his right, while the man who had brought him stood at his left. He heard his guide draw his sword from its sheath. The man on his right now spoke.

'Child of man, I conjure you by the endless circle which comprises all creatures and the highest wisdom, to tell me for what purpose you have come here?'

Michael knew the answer to this, but the solemnity of the situation and the atmosphere in that cold and echoing place filled him with awe.

'To acquire wisdom, art and virtue.'

'Then live,' said the person at his right; the words resonating through the place. Michael gained a sense of a large space, like a church. The voice at his right continued.

'But your spirit must again rule over your body; you have found grace, arise and be free.'

Michael felt the bonds at his wrists untied, and the cord at his throat unloosened and removed. Then, the sack was taken from his head. Michael raised his eyebrows in surprise. He stood in a building of rose-coloured and honey-yellow stone, with columns to right and left, and a high ceiling, decorated with stars, lilies, daisies and roses, was discernible in the light of thirty-three candles. The capitals of the columns were covered with carvings, and each window had carvings right and left, and round the frames. Ahead of him was a curtain, roughly torn down the middle. There were several men in the room, all in black, with black sashes over their shoulders. The man at his right was the elderly man who had interviewed him at the House of the Pelican. He held a white wand, while the guide still held his drawn sword. The two men, standing in the midst of the circle of black-clad men now formed a cross of the wand and the sword, and Michael stepped into the circle. He laid three fingers of his right hand on the point where the sword and wand crossed. He recognized his own sword in the hands of his guide.

'Now listen,' said the old man. 'Do you solemnly swear to have no secrets from the brotherhood?'

'I do,' Michael answered.

'And do you solemnly swear to lead a life of virtue, rendering evil unto no man?'

'I do.'

'Do you see this stone?'

The hierophant stepped back, and those at the eastern end of the chapel stepped back to allow Michael to see a cubic stone; water dripped from one side of it, while the other seemed to be covered in blood. The letter 'J' was carved deeply into it.

'I do see it.'

'What does it signify?'

'The Word that was put to death.'

'The Word that is lost is what you seek. It cannot be given to you. Confusion reigns among us; the veil of the temple is rent; darkness covers the earth. The tools are broken. Yet need you not despair, as we shall find out the new law, that thereby we may recover the lost word. You must travel for thirty-three years.'

One of the black-clad men left the circle. This was the Junior Warden of the Lodge and led Michael round the chapel thirty-three times. On the last circuit, he stopped at the window where a woman was carved, holding a cross, behind a warrior on horseback.

'This is the place of Faith,' said the warden, and pointed to the column opposite the window. 'The most holy Margaret showed in her life and in her actions faith of the most exalted kind, and died in the hope of everlasting reward.'

He led him a short distance across the chapel to a window where a demon held the hem of the garments of a young woman and her child, who turned away from the demon towards an angel, carrying a long-stemmed cross.

'Here is the place of Hope,' said the Warden. 'The hope that we may all, with God's grace, escape the torments of hell, and gain the Life Everlasting.'

The journey continued to the central column, behind which the torn curtain hung.

'This is the place of Love, which we also call Holy Charity,' said the Warden, 'and remember these three, for they must always be your guides.'

The warden now led Michael to the centre, where he was made to kneel with his right knee on a Bible.

'Now repeat after me,' said the hierophant, and his voice became charged with a new gravity. 'I promise never to reveal the secrets of this Lodge, on penalty of being for ever deprived of the True Word; that a river of blood and water shall issue constantly from my body, and under the penalty of suffering anguish of soul, of being steeped in vinegar and gall, of having on my head the most piercing thorns, and of dying upon the cross, so help me the Grand Architect of the Universe.'

Michael repeated the words that the hierophant spoke, hearing his voice echo in that solemn place. Then he was made to rise, and the whole company left the main body of the chapel, and went down into the lower chapel. This room was plain, with nothing of the decoration of the main chapel above. A broad canvas was hung from the eastern wall, painted with a cross surrounded by a glory. At the centre of the cross was a rose. Below the cross were three squares placed at each corner of a triangle, each containing a circle, and in each circle a triangle of equal sides. Crowning the uppermost square was a seven-pointed star, and at the foot of the painting, looking up were an eagle and a pelican, left and right. Below them was painted the tomb with the stone rolled away from the entrance. Thirty-three candles lit the lower chapel. A cubic stone, like the one in the upper chapel, lay on the floor at the centre, beneath the painting.

Michael faced the painting while the black-clad men all spoke the seventeenth chapter of the Gospel of John. Each man had it by heart. They spoke it so that the whole building seemed to tremble at the sound. Michael again felt awestricken, far more so than before.

'Do you know this stone?' asked the hierophant, pointing to the stone cube.

'It is the stone that the builders refused.'

All was going forward as had been described to him, but prepared as he was, his soul felt shivered to its foundations. The worst trial was yet to come.

The High Priestly Prayer, the chapter of John's Gospel having been spoken, the Junior Warden now made his way to a door in the north wall, and opened it. Fear flooded through Michael, though he fought against the feeling. His guide stepped forward from the circle of men, and led him through the door, and sharp left, through a lower door, where all was darkness. Michael went through this shadowy threshold. He became aware of three men lighting seven chandeliers of dimly burning lights that threw a yellow, shuddering light into the chamber. The light gradually revealed a series of stone tables. Suits of armour were laid upon these tables. Michael realized that each suit of armour contained the remains of the man who had worn it. This was the place of the dead. Two men came up behind him, and draped a shroud of black cloth, covered in ashes, over him. Again, he was blind in this dark mausoleum. He felt himself being led round the chamber, and then down a steep slope in the utter darkness. It smelled of earth. Down, down they went into the cold, dank earth. Sometimes his foot slipped, but strong hands kept him upright. Dread began to fill his soul. He tried to counter it by remembering what he had been told in preparation, but the solemnity of the mood and the sense of being on the brink of something momentous made his palm sweat and his heart beat hard and fast.

At last, after what must have been some hundreds of yards, the path downwards came to an end, and the cloth was removed. Michael's heart leaped in his breast as he saw before him three devils, and only slowly did he manage to convince himself that these were men in costume. Here was a room all in shadows, which he had to walk round three times in complete silence. All the while, he tried to remember the three days that Christ spent in hell. Solemn reverence and earthly fear fought for possession of his mind as he made the circuit. Finally, he stood before a black curtain, and the Junior Warden was beside him again.

'The horrors through which you have passed are as nothing compared to the horrors that await you,' Michael was told. He was blindfolded again, and the curtain was lifted. Michael found himself aware through his blindfold that he was in a brightly lit room. The brotherhood was all present.

The hierophant stood before him. Michael strove to recall the words of the catechism that now was to be read out to him.

'Whence come you?'

'From Judea.'

'Which way did you come?'

'By Nazareth.'

'Of what tribe are you descended?'

'Judah.'

'Give me the four initials.'

'I.N.R.I.'

'What do these letters signify?'

'Jesus of Nazareth, King of the Jews.'

'Do they signify anything else?'

'*Iabash, Nuor, Ruach, Iam.*'

'Do you know what these words mean?'

Iabash is the body, fed by the daily bread. *Iam* is the life, and we ask for forgiveness of our life's debts. *Ruach* is the soul that must be kept from temptation, and *Nuor* is the spirit, that must be shielded from evil.'

'Brother,' cried the hierophant in a ringing voice, 'the Word is found. The stone that the builders refused has become the cornerstone of the temple. Let him be restored to light.'

The blindfold was removed. There were no more horrors to be met here. He was in a room that was not in the chapel to which he had been brought. The brotherhood clapped their hands three times, and uttered a loud cheer at each clap.

The mood in the room became more relaxed. Michael was led out of the room by the hierophant, and along a corridor, and into the chilly dawn.

He did not look behind him to see where he had come from, but he was led up a hillside towards the chapel where much of the ceremony that he had undergone had taken place. They entered, and the hierophant took him along the north side of the building, to a carving of an angel in the bottom right corner of the window. The angel held a book closed tight against his breast.

'There are secrets which must be kept,' said the hierophant. 'A lid must be placed on the chalice to keep the wine pure. Is that how you read the carving?'

'I see that,' said Michael, 'and that the book must be kept close to my heart.'

This conversation had had no rehearsal.

'Look up,' said the hierophant, and Michael looking up saw a cross carved in the ceiling, like the many that were carved in the side aisles, but this one had a rose at its centre.

'What does the cross mean to you?' the hierophant asked. Michael was still looking up at it. Finally he lowered his gaze to meet the old man's grey eyes.

'The cross signifies the four elements of which the world is made. But this cross is grailed, the half circles cut all along the cross-pieces are like cups to be filled with the holy blood, just as the world is the bearer of the blood of the great deed of sacrifice.'

'And the rose?'

'The rose appearing at the centre of the cross is a sign of the achievement of the Grail. The body, soul and spirit are so transformed that the blood bears new life, and powers of healing.'

'Yes. It is the flower that blooms only in the darkness of the sanctuary of initiation. It was an object of veneration in Ancient India, in Egypt and in Greece in the olden time. The cross, too, long before it became the sign of the Grand Architect, was the symbol for the world; the four elements coming together at the behest of the gods to create our world.'

He coughed and pursed his lips.

'You were promised further horrors, and yet were given a welcome into the brotherhood. Do you understand this?'

Michael thought for a moment before answering.

'What I went through during the process of initiation was to prepare me for the real dangers on the grail path.'

The old man nodded. He walked towards the pillar in the south east of the chapel, a column carved with garlands wreathed round it in a spiral, their roots each in the mouth of a carved dragon. His age-crooked fingers gently stroked the nearest garland.

'You have taken some strong and binding oaths. Do you wish this transformation?'

Michael looked up at the rose carved in the centre of the cross again.

'I do,' he said fervently. 'I do.'

'The way is long and hard, and beset with doubt, disappointment; even enmity. Do you truly wish it?'

'How can the way be otherwise? Yes. I wish it.'

'The task is to rebuild the temple within yourself. Do you understand this?'

'I am at the beginning of my understanding of it. No more than that.'

The hierophant led Michael outside, and to the eastern wall. There they sat together on a stone bench; part of the fabric of the building. They sat in silence, gazing eastwards, watching the sky gradually grow lighter. A little way before them the ground fell away into a deep glen. Michael could smell the water of a river at the foot, though he could see nothing under the tree canopy, where the shadows of night were still gathered. The hierophant pointed to a star in the east.

'Do you know the name of that star?'

'Of course; it is Venus.'

'When she is the Morning Star, she draws a shape in the heavens, above where the sun rises, in the shape of a horn. When she is the Evening Star, she draws a similar shape in the heavens in the west, after the sun has set. Do you know what we call these horns, east and west?'

Michael remained silent. A breeze ran through the trees of the glen, turning the leaves. It was just light enough to see the different shades of the upper and lower sides of the leaves. The old man turned his grey eyes to him again, and in the growing light, Michael saw how they were strangely youthful.

'We call them the Horns of Isis,' he said. 'Our temple here sits cradled between the Horns of Isis.'

Michael waited, feeling sure that he had something more to say. Sure enough, the old man spoke again.

'When the rose truly appears at the centre of the cross, Isis is no longer widowed.'

Michael turned all of a sudden, startled. His guide stood at his left shoulder, offering him his sword.

'We should go,' he said. 'Two men on one horse might cause a wheen o' blethers. We should be away before the day starts.'

Michael strapped on his sword, and followed him to where the horse was tethered, quietly cropping the grass in the dawn. The topmost folds of the Pentland Hills were already turning gold with the morning light. Birdsong filled the air all around them. He turned once to wave farewell to the hierophant, but he was still gazing into the eastern sky. Of the rest of the brotherhood he saw no trace.

20. The Last of the Templars

'Of course,' Sir Arthur de la Haye said, his voice echoing in the ancient chapel, 'one of the things that the Templars were accused of was recruiting men into their ranks who simply were not worthy of the name Templar. Such men brought the whole Order into disrepute. Some even say that it brought about their downfall.'

The small group that he was guiding nodded wisely, except the little Frenchman, whose face grew troubled.

'The first secular building that the Templars ever constructed was over there, at the village of Temple. The village was called Balantrodoch before that. The name means: "The Place of the Warrior".'

The little group craned round, as though expecting to see the rooftops of Temple appear inside the chapel walls.

'Just the sort of chaps we could have done with at Sebastopol,' said the ex-military man. 'Warriors, I mean.'

Sir Arthur, who had not served in the Crimea, left the remark unanswered.

'Now, we've seen the various signs of the Templars in the chapel,' he continued, his voice echoing among the rosy-pink and honey-coloured stones of the building. 'The Agnus Dei over there; the face on the Veil of Saint Veronica here, and so on. Now I'd like to point out the floriated cross, which we see here, in the ceiling of the north and south aisles.'

He pointed with his stick of Indian ivory, and the little group dutifully looked where he indicated; except a small, dark-haired, nervous-looking man, who watched Sir Arthur closely, with an expression of something like desperate hope. It was not warm in the ancient building. Strong draughts blew in through the cracked and broken glass of the windows, rustling the grasses and weeds that had seeded themselves in the dusty cracks and crevices within the chapel. The moss had grown so thick on some of the carvings of plants that it was impossible to tell at a glance which was living growth, and which the stone.

'Now I want to show you something else, if you'll come with me.'

The group followed Sir Arthur to the north side of the chapel. He stood under a lintel draped with dusty black cobwebs. They squinted in the dim light up into the corner where he pointed his stick.

'It's very dark, but perhaps, I don't know, can you just make out a man here, and a dog that he has on a leash? We ought to have a bull's eye lantern here, eh?'

They craned forward. The old soldier, narrowing his eyes, drawled: 'Oh, yes.'

'Where?' asked a young woman, raising herself on tiptoes. 'Oh! Oh yes! I see it now.'

'That carving represents the Pope, Clement the Fifth as a blind man, being led by Philippe the Fair, the King of France, here shown as a dog. I wish to cause no offence to our French guest, of course.'

Sir Arthur looked at the little man, who shook his head vigorously.

'Ah, *non non non*! No offence at all, I assure you.'

He spoke as if he had a great deal more to say on the matter, but held himself back.

'You'll remember that the Knights Templar, since their humble beginnings in the year 1118, had become a powerful and highly respected Order of monastic knights. They so impressed King David the First that he made them …'

He broke off as a wiry, prematurely aged woman called to him from the door: 'Ah'm no wantin fur tae interrupt ye, nor nothing, Sir Arthur, but ah've mah man's denner tae get, ye ken? It's no fur masel that ah'm askin, ken.'

'All right, Nettie, all right,' Sir Arthur went to the door where she stood, and reached into his pocket, and took out a coin that he hoped was a shilling, but was afraid was a sovereign, and put it discreetly into her hand.

'Now, Nettie, d'ye think your man's dinner can wait a few more minutes?'

'Ach, ah doot he'll girn and complain, but it's a sair fecht onywey,' she said, smiling, and squirreling the coin into the folds of her shawl. 'It's a wee bit mair respect fur his betters he's wantin, ah'm thinkin.'

'Och, ye're a good woman,' Sir Arthur said, and returned to his guests.

He paused to regather his thoughts.

'Yes, the Templars were great builders, farmers, bankers; and held in trust a considerable fortune. They had been the men that all sides trusted during the time of the Crusades, acting as middlemen between men of differing faiths who wished to do business with each other. Many of the architectural concepts and practices of the Gothic style were their own reworkings of what they had seen among the Mohammedans.'

This thought was received with interest, but a slight touch of distaste among some of the group.

'Yes,' said a young man. 'I'd heard that they were the most frightful heretics! The Templars, I mean. They got up to all sorts of …'

He became aware of the young woman, and broke off, embarrassed. The Frenchman looked at Sir Arthur with a knowing smile. Sir Arthur hid his feelings, looking away into a far corner of the chapel.

'They were accused, certainly, of a number of heretical practices, among other, er … But please remember that it was Saint Bernard of Clairvaux, the great Cistercian abbot, who made sure that the Order of the poor Knights of Christ and of the Temple were recognized by and affiliated to the Church of Rome.'

'And, permit me …' the Frenchman broke in, 'these accusations were fabricated by those who wished to see the Knights of the Temple brought into disrepute.' He looked apologetically at Sir Arthur. 'I'm sorry. Please continue.'

'As our friend says, these notions were put about by their enemies, though, of course, we cannot blink the fact that there were among them, men who were not worthy of the Order to which they belonged. Such people gave the whole Order a name for, well, for instance, heresy.'

Sir Arthur pulled the watch from his waistcoat pocket, and looked towards the door, where Nettie sat, waiting for them to leave, so that she could lock the place up and go home to her chores. These people with a taste for the sensational! Well, after all, it *was* sensational; the tortures; the accusations of devil-worship extracted under the Inquisitor's grim will; the slow roasting of the Grand Master of the Order: the prophecy he made before his death and its fulfilment. Yes, there were sensational details enough; and many not for a young woman's ears. He drew a deep breath. It really was time to go. He had trespassed on the good nature of the caretaker of the chapel for too long, and he wished to maintain good relations with her.

'Well, perhaps that is enough for one visit. I should be most happy to answer any questions that you may have …?'

The guests looked at each other. No, there were no questions. It had been a most interesting visit. They thanked Sir Arthur, and left the chapel, making for the nearby hotel, where a large fly waited to take them back to Edinburgh. Only the Frenchman remained behind, looking at the carving of a bearded man, holding an open book and pointing to a page.

'The seventeenth chapter of the Gospel of John, I think? Known in some circles as the High Priestly Prayer,' the Frenchman said. Sir Arthur looked carefully at his guest, and said: 'Yes. I think you know rather a lot about the subject, Monsieur?'

'Forgive me, Sir Arthur, but ...' the Frenchman replied, adding with something of an air of reciting a line of poetry, 'can you tie a bow?'

Sir Arthur laughed aloud in surprise, and gave the answer: 'As well as you.'

The masonic password given and answered; the word 'bow' capped with the word 'as'. Their eyes strayed to ornate pillar at the eastern end of the chapel. It was sometimes referred to as the Boaz pillar, particularly in Masonic circles. They smiled, and their eyes met, Sir Arthur seeing his guest as if for the first time. Then the Frenchman spoke again.

'Sir Arthur, I would like to talk to you, alone, at your convenience, if you would be so good.'

'Well, I, er ...Do you mean now, this minute?'

The Frenchman hesitated.

'I must not impinge on your guests, or your so valuable time, but if now is convenient to you?'

Sir Arthur excused himself for a moment, leaving the little man looking intently at a carving by the north door of the Crucifixion. The cross was not elevated from the rest of the group around it, and only one cross was depicted. It was T-shaped.

'*Mais c'est la mort de Jacques de Molay, bon sang!*' he whispered aloud to himself. '*Il ne s'agit pas du tout de la Crucifixion!*'

He was dimly aware of the voice of Sir Arthur, bidding farewell to his guests. Sir Arthur, his guests now on their way down the road to the hotel nearby, saw the figure of Nettie, pacing to and fro on the grass outside the chapel, a small, chunky dudeen of a clay pipe clamped between her jaws, and her arms tightly folded against her low bosom under the shawl.

'Look, Nettie, d'ye think you could trust me to lock the place up and deliver the key to your house myself? It's just that the foreign gentleman here ...'

She looked at him with wide and solemn eyes.

'Oh, ah'm no very sure, Sir Arthur. It's no me, y'unnerstaun; ah'd gie ye the key and welcome. But ah've the responsibility, ye see.'

Sir Arthur reached into his fob pocket for another coin, which he put carefully into her hand.

'I'll take the responsibility, Nettie. Don't you worry yourself. I'll lock up and bring the key myself to your house. If there's any trouble, I'll bear the row; I've broad enough shoulders for the wrath of the Laird.'

'Well, ah suppose yince'll no dae ony herm. Mind and bring me that key when ye're a' feenished, but! It's mair nor ma life's worth tae loss it!'

She bustled away, her laughter showing no mirth, simply a wish not to offend. Sir Arthur joined the little man in the darkening shadows of the medieval building.

'I think, Sir Arthur, that the democratic spirit is very strong in Scotland, yes?'

Sir Arthur resolutely did not think so.

'Well, we like to think any man can look any other man in the eye, I suppose,' he conceded, 'regardless of rank or station.'

He looked the other in the eye, as if in confirmation. 'Come,' he said, 'let's enjoy the last light outside.'

He carefully locked the door of the chapel, and pocketed the large key. He led the Frenchman to the eastern end of the chapel, where they sat. One star was already visible and bright.

'I should tell you a little about myself, Sir Arthur. I am a Knight of the Temple.'

Sir Arthur said nothing, but briefly tensed and relaxed his arm and shoulder muscles.

'*Non non*, I am not a lunatic, please assure yourself. For over a century now, a group of men has gathered in Paris to dedicate ourselves to the spirit of the Knights of the Temple, who were hunted out of existence in the fourteenth century. It was a quiet affair, as these things should be. But the great Voltaire, he wrote an article in defence of the *Chevaliers du Temple* of old to help to celebrate the refounding of the Order. We are a secular group, but we bind ourselves by the principles of the original *Templier* — how do you say?'

'Templar.'

'Precisely. Some of us even wear the *cordon rouge*, but for others, this is a little too much. Although ...Well, well. We shall come to that'

Sir Arthur cleared his throat, wondering what we should come to, and nodded.

'I assure you, Sir Arthur, we are a group of men who revere the life of the Templars of old, but our meetings are in common more with the freemason. Yes, we use the same calendar as the Templar, the Hebrew lunar calendar; we have different levels of initiation within the order, just as the Temple Knights had them.'

He leaned forward conspiratorially.

'It begins with the recitation of the Lord's Prayer. This is a prayer of the utmost importance to us.'

'Of course,' Sir Arthur said, quietly, but the little man clearly had a great deal to say.

'You understand, Sir Arthur that I tell this to you because, I believe, you are one who can understand this, as a man of honour. I appeal to you as a man of honour.'

Appeal to me, thought Sir Arthur; as a man of honour? This was positively medieval. *Was* the man mad?

'When I joined the Order, I was led to a chamber where stood an altar. I was in no more than a chemise and a light pair of ...'

He indicated his trousers.

'Yes, trousers. Breeches.'

'Thank you, yes, the breeches. Two members of the Order received me in what you call the state of Nature, you understand; nothing on at all.'

The backs of Sir Arthur's hands began to prickle with embarrassment.

'I, er, I hope that this description ...'

The Frenchman was suddenly stern. He rose and looked down fiercely at Sir Arthur.

'Sir Arthur, I tell you this with good reason. Please to listen with close attention. I must tell you these details to prove that I know whereof I speak, and to convince you of the severity of what I must tell.'

'Please carry on,' Sir Arthur said. 'Sorry to interrupt.' He reached for his stick and took it loosely in both hands, holding it between his knees as he sat.

'There is perhaps no need to remind you, Sir Arthur, that there was a saying among stupid people, ignorant people: beware the kiss of the Templars? Yes, it is true that the neophyte is required to kiss the parts of the body that are close to where the chakras lie in the more subtle body?'

'The ...What was it you said? Cha ... Something?'

The Frenchman gestured to his brow, throat, heart, solar plexus, abdomen, but sketched only briefly a movement towards the groin and the base of the spine.

'We are required to overcome the desires of the flesh, Sir Arthur, and to acknowledge that we bear the future within us in our ability to bring children into the world. Never the less, we take a vow of chastity, and leave the fathering of children to other men.'

The little man sighed deeply, and sat again, suddenly looking very tired.

'The initiations continue,' he went on at last, 'all in connection with the Lord's Prayer and certain figures of the New Testament. You may have heard that we spit on the cross?'

'That had come to my ears,' replied the other.

'It is true. But it is to understand fully the state of spirit — am I saying this correctly?'

'State of mind, perhaps, we would say.'

'The state of mind of the Apostle Peter at the moment when he denied Christ. We trample upon a crucifix and spit on it, but we remember the words: *Give us this day our daily bread.* Finally we must look after our earthly bodies. Is it not so? Exactly. And the Hebrew word for this part of the ceremony is *Iabash.* Then follows the next part, in connection with James the Fisherman, and is associated with water, and the source of all life. The Hebrew word is *Iam,* and we remember the words: *Forgive us our debts, as we forgive our debtors.* The next is in memory of the Apostle John, and is connected with the air that we breathe.'

'And I imagine that the word is *Ruach,* is that right?'

'Of course, yes, *Ruach* is the word. And we think the words: *Lead us not into temptation.* The last stage at this level is with Jesus of Nazareth in our minds, and the most spiritual part of our being. The word is *Nuor,*which means fire, and we think to ourselves: Deliver us from evil.'

'Of course,' Sir Arthur interrupted, 'yours isn't the only form of initiation to use these principles, and the Hebrew words. In our own modest ceremonies …'

The Frenchman broke in: 'But naturally. I should be surprised if otherwise was the case. But there are further levels.'

'I don't doubt it, Monsieur, but I wonder whether it were better not to mention them? We tend to be rather discreet about such things, you know.'

Again, the Frenchman leapt to his feet.

'Sir Arthur, you, I know, will understand what I describe here. I do it to give you an earnest of my standing within the Order. If I do not tell you all these things, then what I have to say will have little substance; little meaning. I must persuade you of my ranking in order to tell you what I must. You understand?'

Sir Arthur began to feel less that he was dealing with a maniac. Clearly this man was driven by something that he felt to be of the greatest importance. He would have to hear the man out now, from Christian charity, if from nothing else.

'*Bon*. I continue. From the Cathars of the Languedoc we took the Consolamentum; that is the permission to hear the confession from each other. This is connected with the sign of the Sun. Above this we have the Prayer of Moses. In this ceremony, we give up a little of the hair of our head and beard, and the parings of the nails. This is in the sign of the Moon. Then, at a level still higher, comes the speaking of the High Priestly Prayer, from the Gospel of John. I drew your attention to this in the chapel just now.'

'Yes, indeed. Please go on.'

'The High Priestly Prayer belongs to the sign of Mars, connected with the power of the Word. Now, Sir Arthur, you may have noticed my ring? This is conferred on those who reach to a still higher level. It is said to give one the power of healing, though I am no physician. The words spoken are: *Christus Verus Mercurius Est*. You will understand, of course?'

'Christ is the true Mercury,' Sir Arthur dutifully stated.

'The fifth step is most formidable. The Prayer of Baphomet is spoken in a loud voice. It is shattering to the soul to hear this, Sir Arthur! But it is directed to the Highest and Mightiest Being in the universe, and spoken in the sign of Jupiter. There is a sixth step. This is the anointing of the eyes, in memory of the Magdalene, who anointed the head and feet of Jesus Christ.'

'The sign of Venus, I take it? Do you mind if I smoke a pipe?'

'But not at all, Sir Arthur. Please smoke a pipe. The last step, made in the sign of Saturn … This is most terrible.'

'Please don't distress yourself on my account,' said Sir Arthur, puffing at the freshly lit tobacco. The little man made no sign that he heard.

'It is the revelation of the sign of Baphomet. For some it is permitted to witness a most beautiful head. But for me …'

He fell silent for the space of a minute. Sir Arthur waited for him to speak, his pipe drawing sweetly.

'For me, it was the Black Grail.'

Sir Arthur felt a spasm of nausea grip him. He slowly leaned forward and knocked the burning tobacco out of his pipe.

'I'm not sure that I … Not sure I entirely follow.'

'The head of the Baptist on a silver dish; it is the sign of the evil of which men are capable; the depths to which we may fall.'

He fell silent.

'Yes,' said Sir Arthur uneasily. 'I'm aware of these stages. Beyond that you cannot go. Not any more.'

'*Exactement!* This is so. Because the very highest initiation of the Knights of the Temple was given back to the world of the spirit by Jacques de Molay himself, before his arrest, in a ceremony in reverse. But this you perhaps knew?'

'I had heard a waif word on the topic.'

'Yes, yes. All the initiations that we follow, we do so because the original Templars followed precisely these rituals. This you know, of course. Sir Arthur, do you know why I come here? To this very place?'

'I should be most interested to learn, Monsieur.'

'I needed to know that there is a place on this earth where the true ideals of the Templar Knights are held in reverence. In this little chapel, built a century after the demise of the Order of the Temple, I find this place. Here the truth lies.'

He leaned forward, taking his head in his hands, sighing deeply.

'Ah, *mon Dieu, mon Dieu! C'est terrible!*'

'You seem distressed, Monsieur. Is there anything I can do?'

'Yes, Sir Arthur! You can do me the greatest honour by listening to my tale.'

The light was fading fast now. A couple was toiling up the hill from the glen below them, lost in tender conversation. Sir Arthur wanted to look at his watch, but did not want to offend the little man. The heavy key was a weight in his pocket that he longed to hand over.

'Well, is it very long?'

'Permit me, Sir Arthur, I will be as brief as possible. *Bon*. My role in the order in Paris is to be the secretary. I must take full notes of our meetings, and offer them as a true document of what has happened.

'It is now some months that we chose a new Grand Master. He is most efficient; he seemed to us a man of honour. But one day, he calls me to his office. Of course, I go. It is part of my duty, to obey in every request the *Grand Maître*. He tells to me that our most important text now, to which we all show honour and reverence, is the *Levitikon*.'

'The what?'

'This is the Gospel of John, Sir Arthur, but not the one that you and I know. This is the Gospel of John with the final two chapters excised. Erased.'

'Without the last two chapters? Oh, no; that won't do! That's not right at all!'

'Ah, Sir Arthur, you think the same as me. What is the Gospel of John if it says nothing of the Resurrection? This is not, as you say, right at all. For me, the English phrase is most apt: the abomination of desolation! Yet this is the text that we are now expected to hold as most sacred; the text that is robbed of its sacred character!'

'So, what did you do?'

'I said nothing! I was too astonished to speak. But now he says to me that I must go through the documents of our meetings, as far as the beginning, and make alterations that indicate that this *Levitikon* was at all times our most sacred text! For me this is blasphemy! But what can I do? I must obey the *Grand Maître, n'est-ce pas?*'

Sir Arthur felt a chill across his shoulders and a hollowness in his breast. He understood the little man's need to talk, the look of desperate hope. Deliberate falsification of the minutes of the meetings of this quasi-masonic group may have seemed a trifling affair to the outside world, but he understood the enormity of it: powerful men denying the truth of the central event of what, on the face of it, drew them together. It meant that this group was now acting absolutely counter to their professed aims. There were men in the world claiming the name of Templar Knights, following their rituals and ceremonies, but dedicated to aims entirely opposite to the high and selfless ideals of the first bearers of the name Templar Knights.

'You are obviously a man of conscience, Monsieur. How did you go forward?'

'This is what I did. I demanded a court of the order to hear my case, and to give a judgment. This they did. It took a long time to convene. The Grand Masters of all Europe and of America had to be there, or at least, represented.'

'Of all Europe? Of the United States? This is a large organization, I gather!'

'It began in Paris, and has spread across the world, Sir Arthur. So, I make my case to the Masters. They tell me that I shall hear a ruling from them in the fullness of time. Meanwhile, I come to this little chapel to refresh my faith and to give more strength to my conscience. Here, in this place, I feel at peace, at least. I must put my faith in the judgment of the *Grands Maîtres*. What else can I do? I can do no other.'

'Well,' said Sir Arthur slowly, 'I'm glad to hear it. Your task has been a difficult one, Monsieur, and I applaud your strength of character.'

He stood, and offered his hand. The little man took it and shook it warmly.

'Thank you for listening to me, Sir Arthur. It is a comfort to me that at least one man knows the truth; a man of honour, such as you are yourself. If you don't mind, I shall remain here for a little. It is so peaceful, and the truth of centuries is in these old stones.'

Sir Arthur made his way towards Nettie's house to return the key. In the lane below the chapel, he passed two men. As he approached, one of them drew the other in to the side of the road, but the other shook his head, and they continued. Were they looking for him? No, obviously not. He passed them, greeting them as he did so. Their reply was no more than a grunt from one, and silence from the other.

A group of men, an international group, men with power and influence, presumably, were behaving in this manner? It didn't bear thinking about. What was his phrase? The abomination of desolation. Now, where did he know that expression from? He felt in his pocket for his pipe. It was there, the bowl still warm, but he left it there.

He handed the key over to Nettie, who came to the door smoothing her apron and smiling with embarrassment, and he made his way to the hotel. As he stood at the door of the entrance to the bar, he heard a cry, as of a dog, or a fox or something, probably from somewhere in the glen, behind the chapel. It was strange how human they could sound sometimes. He entered, closing the door behind him against the cold.

Epilogue

The Egyptians taught us to look at signs and symbols in a threefold way: to look for the earthly meaning, the spiritual meaning and the divine. Names, too, have their levels of meaning: Noah was also called Menachem; Elijah also had the identity of Naboth, while Solomon had seven names in all. So it is with Rosslyn. No picture, no carving has a single meaning once and for all. Even the chapel itself has layers of meaning. The name Rosslyn itself has many meanings. It is the place of the Rose-Line for some. For others it is the Ros-linn, the dew pool. For others again, it is the place of ancient knowledge, and for others again, it is the place by the wood. Each of these names, and others not mentioned here, is true.

It is currently a Scottish Episcopalian Church, and serves that purpose for its congregation. Once it was a Roman Catholic Church. Its function as a Christian church is long established, and has been the place of worship for thousands of people through the time of its consecration. Through the period of its long silence, from the Reformation to its re-consecration in the nineteenth century, it still held an attraction for those with a sense of mystery. That attraction still exists, and is well-known today. The number of tourists who visit Rosslyn still runs into thousands each year.

As the congregation enters Rosslyn today, perhaps some of them can feel the shadow of the old Mithras initiation, for, as we have said, Rosslyn is built on the site of an old subterranean temple of Mithras. We drew attention to the connection between the life of Elijah and the Mithras initiation earlier in this work. Perhaps other, more recent forms of illumination cast their spell, too. It is entirely in keeping with the spirit of Rosslyn that we can associate her with influences as diverse as the Mithras worship of the Roman military and the life of an Old Testament prophet, before even entering the building.

But while it serves the Scottish Episcopalian congregation as the Collegiate Church of Saint Matthew, it is also a structure that transcends the limits of any single denomination. Rosslyn is inclusive. The Manicheans and the Templars, both condemned as heretics, are honoured here. The architecture of the building shows the influence, as does all Gothic architecture, of the influence of Islam; the Gothic arch is a metamorphosis of forms of Moslem buildings seen by the Templars in the Middle East in the time of the Crusades. Judaism is given the place that it must have in any Christian place of worship, particularly in the north aisle, but elsewhere, too. Many have seen the influence of the Cabbalah, the esoteric Judaic tradition, in the forms and structures of Rosslyn, and it would be consistent with the inclusive nature of Rosslyn for this to be so. The qualities of the Sephirotic Tree of Cabbalah each find their reflection in the carvings in the chapel, but let us leave that for other researchers to elucidate.

The world that was known to William Sinclair, Elizabeth Douglas and Gilbert de la Haye is represented in Rosslyn, and the history of that world as they knew it; in particular, the spiritual history.

Rosslyn is a temple dedicated to the striving of all people of all time to raise and transform the physical into the spiritual. The various stories that the carvings and windows illustrate show this. It was the meaning of the task laid upon Adam and Eve at the expulsion from Eden, and all who followed them. It was for a long time, according to the various myths, the province of the descendants of Cain, but became universal with the building of the first temple of Solomon. The transformation of stones into a temple was the metaphor for the transformation of the human being into a being of spirit. 'Destroy this temple,' said Jesus according to the Gospel of John, 'and I shall rebuild it in three days.' He was understood to be talking about the temple of Solomon, which had taken the same length of time to build as Rosslyn, some forty years; but such was not His meaning.

When looked at in isolation, the history of any religion shows absurdities and superstition and the machinations of corrupt men, as well as its beauties, and the spiritual comfort that it may have brought to many. But this will always be limited. Take all religions together and we see a great evolution. Elements that were disparate and isolated become part of a greater picture, ever changing, ever evolving, but only making full sense as a whole.

Rosslyn, held together with the mortar of the steadfast dedication of pilgrims, nestling between the Horns of Isis, is a monument to the striving of all humanity towards something greater than itself which is nevertheless native to itself. We can see where we have come from, looking back over the vast ages of history. Are there still things to discover about the human being? Have we truly evolved as far as we can, or is there more to the story? The mask of Hermes Trismegistus in the east of the chapel, with the triple diadem that grows from the transformation of forces latent in the soul, is the answer that Rosslyn gives us: human evolution is not yet accomplished, but any future growth, any transformation of the human being into new possibilities, must be chosen and willed by us.

However, to understand this extraordinary building in its fullness, we must be ready to be flexible in our reading of its symbolism, in the way of the Ancient Egyptians. The stories here are only one approach. Others will no doubt have other stories about Rosslyn to tell: the book is not finished; only closed for the time being.

The Book closed.

Sources and Further Reading

Introduction
The Holy Blood and the Holy Grail, Michael Baigent, Richard Leigh & Henry Lincoln (1982), Jonathan Cape, London.
Rosslyn — A History of the Guilds, the Masons and the Rosy Cross, Robert Brydon (1994), Friends of Rosslyn, Edinburgh.
Rosslyn and the Western Mystery Tradition, Robert Brydon (2003), Ross Publishing, East Kilbride.
Rosslyn Revealed, Alan Butler & John Ritchie (2006), O Books, Winchester UK.
Scottish Architecture 1371–1560, Richard Fawcett (1994), Edinburgh University Press.
The Tree of Life and the Holy Grail, Sylvia Francke (2007), Temple Lodge Press, Forest Row.
The Hiram Key, Christopher Knight & Robert Lomas (1996), Arrow Books, UK.
Rosslyn Chapel, Angelo Maggi (2008), Birlinn, Edinburgh.
Rosslyn and the Grail, Mark Oxbrow & Ian Robertson (2005), Mainstream, Edinburgh.
The Spiritual Purpose to Rosslyn, Jackie Queally (2007), privately published.
The Spiritual meaning of Rosslyn's Carvings, Jackie Queally (2007), privately published.
Rosslyn, Andrew Sinclair (2005), Birlinn, Edinburgh.
The Secret Scroll, Andrew Sinclair (2001), Sinclair-Stevenson, UK.
Deeper Secrets of Human History, Rudolf Steiner: Lectures from 1909 (1995), Anthroposophic Press, New York.
The Origins of Freemasonry, David Stevenson (1988)), Cambridge University Press.
The Illustrated Guide to Rosslyn Chapel and Castle, Hawthornden, etc., The Rev John Thomson (2003), Masonic Publishing Co. Glasgow.
Rosslyn, Guardian of the Secrets of the Holy Grail, Tim Wallace-Murphy & Marilyn Hopkins (1999), Thorsons, London.
The Templar Legacy and the Masonic Inheritance within Rosslyn Chapel, Tim Wallace-Murphy (1994), The Friends of Rosslyn, Roslin.
The Journals of Dorothy Wordsworth, Dorothy Wordsworth, Ed. Colette Clark (1978), Penguin, UK.

Chapter 1
Mimekor Yisrael, Micha Joseph bin Gorion (1990), Indiana University Press.
Genesis, Creation and the Patriarchs, Emil Bock (1983), Floris Books, Edinburgh.
Genesis, Rudolf Steiner: Lectures from 1910 (1959), Rudolf Steiner Press, London.

Chapter 2
The Temple Legend, Rudolf Steiner: Lectures from 1904, 1906 (1985), Rudolf Steiner Press, London.
The Tree of Life and the Holy Grail, Sylvia Francke.
The Legend of the Rood, F.E. Halliday (trans.) (1955), Duckworth, London.

Chapter 3
Myths of the World, Padraic Colum (2002), Floris Books, Edinburgh.
Ancient Myths and the New Isis Mystery, Rudolf Steiner: Lectures from 1918, 1920 (1994), Anthroposophic Press, New York.
Rosslyn and the Grail, Mark Oxbrow & Ian Robertson.
Myths and Legends of Egypt, Lewis Spence (1994), Senate Books, London.
Sun Songs, Raymond van Over (ed.) (1980), New American Library, New York.

Chapter 4
The Great Initiates, Édouard Schuré (1961), Harper & Row, San Francisco.
Ancient Myths and the New Isis Mystery, Rudolf Steiner: Lectures from 1918, 1920.

Chapter 5
Genesis, Emil Bock.
Genesis, Rudolf Steiner: Lectures from 1910.
Mimekor Yisrael, Micha Joseph bin Gorion.

Chapter 6
Moses, Emil Bock (1986), Floris Books, Edinburgh.
The Great Initiates, Édouard Schuré.
Mimekor Yisrael, Micha Joseph bin Gorion.
The Sign and the Seal, Graham Hancock (1992), William Heinemann, London.

Chapter 7
The Book of Esdras, The Apocrypha Cambridge University Press.
Kings and Prophets, Emil Bock (1989), Floris Books, Edinburgh.
The Hiram Key, Christopher Knight & Robert Lomas.
The Book of Hiram, Christopher Knight & Robert Lomas (2003), Arrow Books, London.
The Temple Legend, Rudolf Steiner: Lectures from 1904, 1906.

Chapter 8
Kings and Prophets, Emil Bock.
Mimekor Yisrael, Micha Joseph bin Gorion.

Chapter 9
The Childhood of Jesus, Emil Bock (1997), Floris Books, Edinburgh.
Christmas Plays from Oberufer, A.C. Harwood (trans.) (1944), Rudolf Steiner Press, London.
The Gospel of Saint Matthew, Rudolf Steiner: Lectures from 1910 (1965), Rudolf Steiner Press, London.

Chapter 10
Christ Legends and Other Stories, Selma Lagerlöf (1977), Floris Books, Edinburgh.
Secrets of the Stations of the Cross, Judith von Halle (2007), Temple Lodge Press, Forest Row.

Chapter 11
Secrets of the Stations of the Cross, Judith von Halle.
The Spear of Destiny, Trevor Ravenscroft (1973), G.P. Putnam's, New York.
The Ninth Century, W.J. Stein (1991), Temple Lodge Press, Forest Row.

Chapter 12
The Spiritual Meaning of Rosslyn's Carvings, Jackie Queally.

Chapter 13
The Religion of the Manichees, Fr Burkitt S.J. (1924), Cambridge University Press.
The Secret Heresy of Hieronymus Bosch, Lynda Harris (1995), Floris Books, Edinburgh.
Mani, his life and work, Richard Seddon (1998), Temple Lodge Press, London.
The Genius of Mani, Andrew Welburn (in *Journal for Anthroposophy* 38).
Manichean Writings, Andrew Welburn*(ibid.).*

Chapter 14
The History of the Kings of Britain, Geoffrey of Monmouth (trans. Lewis Thorpe) (1966), Penguin, London.
Arthur and the Lost Kingdoms, Alistair Moffat (1999), Weidenfeld & Nicholson, London.
The Mystery of Arthur at Tintagel, Richard Seddon (1990), Rudolf Steiner Press, London.
From Round Table to Holy Grail, Isabel Wyatt (1979), Lanthorn Press, East Grinstead.
The Death of Merlin, W.J. Stein (1989), Floris Books, Edinburgh.

Chapter 15
The Arcana of the Holy Grail, John Barnwell (1999), Verticordia Press, USA.
Parzival and Titurel, Wolfram von Eschenbach (trans. Cyril Edwards) (2004), Oxford University Press.
Perceval, Chrétien de Troyes (trans. William W. Kibler) (1991), Penguin, London.
The Ninth Century, W.J. Stein.
Knowledge of Higher Worlds, Rudolf Steiner (1969), Rudolf Steiner Press.
The Speech of the Grail, Linda Sussman (1995), Lindisfarne Press, New York.

Chapter 16
Queen Margaret of Scotland, Eileen Dunlop (2005), NMSE Publishing, Edinburgh.
A History of Scotland, J.D. Mackie (1964), Penguin, London.
Margaret Queen of Scotland, Alan J. Wilson (2001), John Donald, Edinburgh.

Chapter 17
The Hiram Key, Christopher Knight & Robert Lomas.
The Rise and Fall of the Knights Templar, Gordon Napier (2003), Spellmount, Staplehurst.
The Knights Templar, Rudolf Steiner: Lectures compiled and edited by Margaret Jonas (2007), Rudolf Steiner Press, London.

Chapter 18
Robert the Bruce's Forgotten Victory, Graham Bell (2005), Tempus Publishing, London.
A History of Scotland, J.D. Mackie.
The Origins of Freemasonry, David Stevenson.

Chapter 19
The Secret Societies of All Ages and Countries, Charles W. Heckethorn (1897), University Books, New York.

Chapter 20
Histoire de la Condamnation d'un Templier, Anonymous, Ed. Christian Lacour-Ollé (2000), Rediviva, Nîmes.

Chartres

Sacred Geometry, Sacred Space

Gordon Strachan

Gordon Strachan, author of the highly acclaimed *Jesus the Master Builder* (Floris Books, 1998), is back with a ground-breaking new work.

In this book he explores the magnificent structure of Chartres Cathedral, and examines the influences on the medieval master builders.

Using Chartres as a starting point, Dr Strachan suggests that the origins of the Gothic style may lie in Islamic architecture. He goes on to consider how the experience of a particular architectural space affects us, and how sacred geometry works.

Beautifully illustrated in a large format, this is an inspiring and informative book for anyone interested in religious architecture and spirituality.

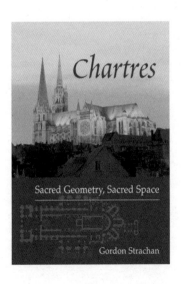

www.florisbooks.co.uk

Prophets of Nature

Green Spirituality in Romantic Poetry and Painting

Gordon Strachan

Many millennia before the present Scriptures existed, God wrote his first book, namely, nature itself. It was through this 'original Bible' that men and women of ancient times experienced the mind and will of God. It then seemed as if the eighteenth century intellectual Enlightenment closed that book forever. However in the following century, the Romantic poets and painters rediscovered the spirit enshrined in the natural world.

This perceptive study, by well-known thinker and writer Gordon Strachan, discusses the tradition of green spirituality as seen through poets such as Wordsworth and Coleridge, and painters such as Samuel Palmer, Caspar David Friedrich and William Turner.

Strachan argues for the genuine spiritual vision of these artists before the so-called twilight of Romanticism set in. He shows that there are many deep springs of inspiration in their work which chime with our current environmental concerns.

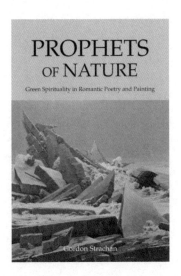

www.florisbooks.co.uk

Patterns of Eternity

Sacred Geometry and the Starcut Diagram

Malcolm Stewart

Malcolm Stewart has discovered a remarkable geometrical device. The 'starcut diagram', as he has called it, is at first glance a simple way of dividing the area of a square. After extensive research, however, he found that it has extraordinary mathematical properties, suggesting that it may be no less than the source of the number system used when ancient humanity first built cities.

He shows that the starcut diagram underlies many significant patterns and proportions across the world: in China, the shaman's dance; in Egypt, the Great Pyramid; in Europe, a Raphael fresco; in Asia, the Vedic Fire Altar, and many others.

This book is an intellectual adventure, written for a general reader without specialist knowledge. Illustrated with around 180 photographs, drawings and diagrams, it tells the story of many fresh discoveries, bringing sacred geometry to life in an original and inspiring way.

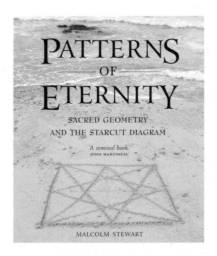

www.florisbooks.co.uk